"I Missed Seeing You Pregnant," Jeff Said. "I'm Betting You Looked Beautiful."

Kelly laughed and tried to take a step back. But he wrapped his arms around her middle and held on for all he was worth.

Jeff looked down into her irresistible green eyes and, even in the dim light, he saw his future. He'd listened to her talk about her brothers, about the strength of the bond between them, and he'd hungered at the love in her voice. He'd watched her with them, with his daughter, and longed to be included in the easy give and take of a family. Even more than he had when he was a kid, standing on the outside of warmth, looking in.

Then it was just a sense of wanting to belong— *anywhere*. Now he wanted to belong with Kelly. He wanted to be a part of her warm and generous heart.

This wasn't just about their child.

He was in love. For the first and last time in his life. And he wanted it all…desperately!

Dear Reader,

Welcome to the world of Silhouette Desire, where you can indulge yourself every month with romances that can only be described as passionate, powerful and provocative!

The ever-fabulous Ann Major offers a *Cowboy Fantasy,* July's MAN OF THE MONTH. Will a fateful reunion between a Texas cowboy and his ex-flame rekindle their fiery passion? In *Cherokee,* Sheri WhiteFeather writes a compelling story about a Native American hero who, while searching for his Cherokee heritage, falls in love with a heroine who has turned away from hers.

The popular miniseries BACHELOR BATTALION by Maureen Child marches on with *His Baby!*—a marine hero returns from an assignment to discover he's a father. The tantalizing Desire miniseries FORTUNES OF TEXAS: THE LOST HEIRS continues with *The Pregnant Heiress* by Eileen Wilks, whose pregnant heroine falls in love with the investigator protecting her from a stalker.

Alexandra Sellers has written an enchanting trilogy, SONS OF THE DESERT: THE SULTANS, launching this month with *The Sultan's Heir.* A prince must watch over the secret child heir to the kingdom along with the child's beautiful mother. And don't miss Bronwyn Jameson's Desire debut—an intriguing tale involving a self-made man who's *In Bed with the Boss's Daughter.*

Treat yourself to all six of these heart-melting tales of Desire—and see inside for details on how to enter our Silhouette Makes You a Star contest.

Enjoy!

Joan Marlow Golan

Joan Marlow Golan
Senior Editor, Silhouette Desire

Please address questions and book requests to:
Silhouette Reader Service
U.S.: 3010 Walden Ave., P.O. Box 1325, Buffalo, NY 14269
Canadian: P.O. Box 609, Fort Erie, Ont. L2A 5X3

His Baby!
MAUREEN CHILD

Published by Silhouette Books

America's Publisher of Contemporary Romance

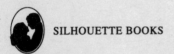

SILHOUETTE BOOKS

ISBN 0-373-76377-8

HIS BABY!

Books by Maureen Child

Silhouette Desire

Have Bride, Need Groom #1059
The Surprise Christmas Bride #1112
Maternity Bride #1138
The Littlest Marine #1167
The Non-Commissioned Baby #1174
The Oldest Living Married Virgin #1180
Colonel Daddy #1211
Mom in Waiting #1234
Marine under the Mistletoe #1258
The Last Santini Virgin #1312
The Next Santini Bride #1317
Marooned with a Marine #1325
Prince Charming in Dress Blues #1366
His Baby! #1377

*Bachelor Battalion

MAUREEN CHILD

was born and raised in Southern California and is the only person she knows who longs for an occasional change of season. She is delighted to be writing for Silhouette Books and is especially excited to be a part of the Desire line.

An avid reader, Maureen looks forward to those rare rainy California days when she can curl up and sink into a good book. Or two. When she isn't busy writing, she and her husband of twenty-five years like to travel, leaving their two grown children in charge of the neurotic golden retriever who is the *real* head of the household. Maureen is also an award-winning historical writer under the names of Kathleen Kane and Ann Carberry.

SILHOUETTE MAKES YOU A STAR!

Feel like a star with Silhouette.
Look for the exciting details of our new contest
inside all of these fabulous Silhouette novels:

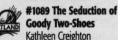

One

In the moonless night, bullets bit into the ground and snatched at the bushes and trees around him. Jeff Hunter knew the enemy was firing blind. They sure as heck couldn't see him, hidden as he was. But that didn't mean that one of them couldn't get lucky.

He kept his head down and a tight grip on his weapon as he used his elbows and knees to move closer to shore. To the boat that was waiting for him. The rest of his Recon team was already on board, he knew. He was the last man out. As always.

As the next in a series of explosions rocked the night, Jeff grinned briefly and kept going. Elbows, knees, through the plants, closer to escape. He didn't look back. Didn't have to. He knew his job and did it well. Everything was blowing up right on schedule. Flames lit the darkness, and flickering shadows jumped around him like shadows of the damned. Mission accomplished, he thought and shifted his focus from the job to the matter at hand—getting the hell out of Dodge.

Belly-crawling faster now, he ignored the slap of bullets, the roar of the inferno behind him and the frantic shouts of the enemy as they searched for him. Slipping out of the tangled undergrowth to the sand, he rolled, came up onto his feet and crouching, dashed the last few feet to the boat. Here it was most dangerous. Here he was unprotected by the foliage. A straight, clean stretch of beach lay between him and safety, and Jeff set a new world's record in running while bent nearly in half. Instinct drove him and he ducked as a couple more charges were detonated, crashing into the hot night air.

Even as he rushed clumsily through knee-deep water and dived headfirst into the safety of the rubber Zodiac boat, the outboard motor was firing up. Eager hands reached for him, grabbing hold of his Kevlar vest and yanking him the rest of the way into the boat. He lay flat for a long minute, catching his breath. Safety. His team members. His friends. Hell, his family.

"Called it close enough that time, Gunny," Deke muttered, shoving the throttle forward and sending the Zodiac into a screaming takeoff that left white foam plumes of water in its wake.

Damn, but that engine sounded good. They'd had to row in when they'd arrived, but now, it didn't matter how much noise they made. Get in quiet—get out fast.

He slanted the other man a look and smiled. Shouting to be heard over the full-out motor, he said, "Yeah, yeah. Quit whining. You ladies were safe in the boat while I'm out saving the world for humanity."

Deke laughed, throwing his head back and whooping a little just to celebrate surviving.

"Oh, I like that," J.T. quipped loudly, "here we sit around waitin' for him—lookin' like targets a boot recruit couldn't miss and he insults us."

"Yeah," Travis drawled, keeping his mounted gun trained on the retreating shore to cover their escape, just in case some of the enemy survived all of the explosions and were just a bit testy. "Sounds to me like the Gunny's getting a little cocky in his old age. Maybe we ought to throw him out and make him swim.''

Deke steered for the ship waiting just out of sight around a point of land a few miles off the starboard bow. ''Nah,'' he countered, gaze locked ahead, ''some shark would take a bite out of him and get poisoned. Doesn't seem fair to the fish.''

Jeff chuckled to himself and lay back. The other guys had it handled. In a few short minutes, they'd be picked up by the ship, and five days from now, they'd all be on leave.

Their first leave in way too long.

The moon peeked out from behind a trail of clouds, and in the brief flash of silvery moonlight, Jeff looked at the faces around him. Camouflage paint obscured their features as well as his, and their eyes and teeth shone weirdly against the darkness. Jokes aside, he'd trust any one of them with his life. And had. Too many times to count.

Then his gaze shifted to the other man in the boat. The reason for the team's presence. The man they'd been sent in to rescue.

Some diplomat who'd stayed too long in an unfriendly country and worn out his welcome, he'd been taken hostage a month ago. No doubt he'd given up hope of ever going home again. Until Deke had slit open the back of the guy's tent and whispered, "U.S. Marines." Hell, the man had nearly wept and Jeff was pretty sure if he'd been able to, he would have given them a brass-band welcome.

Now he sat, leaning forward in the boat, as if reaching toward home would get him there faster. And that was okay by Jeff, since he was in a hurry to get back to the States, too. It had been eighteen months since his last real leave. Eighteen months since he'd last seen Kelly.

In the darkness with only the hum of the engines and the distant roar of explosions breaking the silence, Jeff relaxed for the first time in ten hours and let his mind wander. Back to that night. The last one he'd spent with the woman who now haunted his every dream.

Kelly reached for him and he pulled her close, relishing the feel of her warm, naked flesh against his. It had been a hell of a two-week leave. Starting with that first day, when he'd pulled her, unconscious, from the ocean after a loose surfboard conked her on the head.

Once on shore, he'd given her mouth-to-mouth and they'd pretty much been that way ever since. He'd never experienced anything like it before.

Such a rush of emotion. Such a tangle of feelings. Such incredible want and need.

And now it was their last night together. He'd be shipping out in the morning, headed who knew where. And when he'd be back, even he didn't know. He held her tighter, closer, in response to that thought and tried to block out the image of goodbye.

"These two weeks went so fast," she murmured, and her breath dusted across his skin. Her fingers trailed through the dark hair on his chest, and his breath caught at the fire in her touch.

"Yeah," he said, inhaling the light, flowery scent of her hair, "it did."

She tipped her head back to look up at him. "How early do you have to leave?"

In the soft haze of candlelight, her long, curly auburn hair looked golden, streaks of light and dark color coming together to blend into a whole that made him think of fires at night. So soft, so... "Early," he said. "Have to be on base at six."

She looked past him at the digital alarm clock on her bedside table. "It's only midnight. We still have hours."

"Not nearly enough time," he said, knowing it for fact. But then if he had fifty years at his disposal, he didn't think it would be enough time.

There was something about this woman that made him want to forget everything else in the world existed. He'd like nothing more than to lock them both inside this room and stay there.

But that just wasn't an option. So instead, he resolved to make the most of what time they had left. To not waste it in wishing for what couldn't be. He cupped her face in his palm and stroked the pad of his thumb across her cheek. Then shifting, he rolled to one side and levered himself up over her. He looked down into those forest-green eyes of hers and asked, "You gonna miss me?"

One corner of her mouth twitched into a crooked smile. "I might," she said softly, running her hands up and down his back with feather-light strokes that fired the need coiled dangerously inside him. "But maybe you should remind me again just what it is I'm going to miss."

"Oh," he said, sliding one hand down to cup her breast, "I think I could do that." His thumb and forefinger tugged at her nipple, and he smiled when she arched into his touch, tipping her head back into the pillow.

"Okay," she said on a sigh, "it's coming back to me now."

The words hung in the air for a long minute, and he waited until her eyes were open again and she was looking at him. Then he said in a low, throaty growl, "I'm coming back to you, too, Kelly. Not sure when. But I'll be back."

She took his face in her hands and pulled him close. "Promise?"

He turned his face into her hand and kissed her palm. "Oh yeah, baby. I promise."

Then he kissed her, drowning in the taste of her, silently telling himself to remember. Remember it all. Her scent, her touch, her taste. He wanted it all so clear in his mind that no matter where he was or what he was doing, he'd be able to bring this moment back.

She sighed and he caught that small, escaped breath and drew it down deep inside him, taking a part of her into himself. Tongues met and clashed, tangling together as the fire grew and threatened to devour both of them.

His hands moved over her curves, defining them, burning them into his memory. He felt her slide one hand across his back, down along his spine to his butt, then around, to cup him in her palm. His eyes squeezed closed and his back teeth ground together as he fought for control. But her hands on him were too much and she damn well knew it. When she shifted, encircling the length of him with her fingers, he growled from low in his throat and caught her hand, drawing it up to the pillow beside her head and pinning it there.

"Problem?" she asked, with a spark of knowing innocence in her eyes.

"No problem here," he told her, and moved to cover her body with his.

"Glad to hear it." She moved beneath him, parting her legs, lifting her hips in welcome.

Jeff accepted that invitation and pushed himself into the deep warmth of her. As her body surrounded him and her hands came up to encircle his neck, he rocked his hips against her. Retreat and advance. He moved within her, pushing them both higher, faster as they rushed together toward the completion that lay just out of reach.

He'd found something here. With her. Something unexpected. Something he wasn't quite sure what to do about. Something he knew he didn't want to lose, yet something he was going to have to leave.

His brain raced; every nerve ending in his body hummed. Then she clutched at his shoulders and held on for dear life, and he felt her body tremble and convulse just a moment before his own world erupted. And in that blinding flash, Jeff knew that being apart from her would be the most difficult thing he'd ever done.

* * *

And it had been. It had been a hell of a long eighteen months. But he *was* going back. He was keeping that promise to return. He only hoped she gave a damn. Wouldn't it be a kick in the ass if he'd been thinking about her all this time and she hadn't given him a single thought?

The Zodiac gun boat collided with the side of the destroyer, and the solid bump jolted Jeff from his wandering thoughts.

A rope ladder dropped from above, and as J.T. and Travis helped the diplomat clamber to safety, Deke looked over at Jeff and asked, "Thinking about that woman again, Gunny?"

Jeff shot his friend a look. Shouldn't be surprised at the comment, he thought. The guys had heard plenty about Kelly on those long nights of inaction while waiting for the hoo-ha to start.

"Beats the hell out of thinking about you guys."

"Guess so," Deke acknowledged with a grin. Then he asked, not for the first time, "At least the way you tell it. So, this redhead of yours have any sisters?"

"Don't know," Jeff said, silently admitting that they'd never really gotten around to talking about family. They'd been way too busy with each other. "But I'll let you know."

"Good enough," Deke said, and grabbed a handful of rope. "Five days and a wakeup and we'll be stateside again."

Jeff glanced at his watch. Ten minutes past midnight. "*Four* days and a wakeup," he corrected, and slung his weapon onto his back before climbing the ropes. Four more days, he told himself. Then he'd wake up, grab the first flight to California and be knocking on Kelly's door.

He swung his legs over the rail and clambered aboard. Good to feel solid ship under his feet again. Then, as he helped the swabbies pull the Zodiac out of the water, his brain started that slow wander again.

After eighteen months of sending her postcards and one too brief phone call, he'd be able to hold her, kiss her, taste her again. And he figured this time, maybe he *would* lock them both into her bedroom and not come out till they were starving to death.

Kelly Rogan stared at the latest postcard from Jeff Hunter. It had been mailed more than two weeks ago—from where, she wasn't sure. He never told her where he was. Apparently that was a big no-no, militarywise. But occasionally she could figure it out from the picture on the card. Like say, the one she'd received with a lovely shot of the Eiffel Tower. But this one was simply palm trees and sandy beaches. Heck, that could mean anything from Hawaii to Fiji to Vietnam.

But it didn't really matter, did it? It was what he'd written on the back that was important. She flipped it over and read again the words she already knew by heart.

Coming home. Be there by the end of March.
Have thirty days leave. Can't wait to see you.

Jeff

End of March. That meant he'd be here any day now. And Kelly wasn't at all sure how she felt about that. After all, his last two-week leave had changed her life forever.

Too many times in the past eighteen months she'd played the what-if game. What if she hadn't gone surfing that day? What if Jeff hadn't been the one to save her? What if she hadn't looked up into those blue eyes of his?

What if—?

Well, that was a pointless game anyway. She *had* gone surfing. She *had* nearly drowned. Jeff *had* rescued her. And for the first time in her noneventful life, Kelly had given into spontaneity.

She'd lived in the moment. She'd had a two-week-long, incredibly passionate affair with a tall, dark stranger. And the rest, as they say, was history.

All that mattered now was facing Jeff and telling him what she'd been unable to tell him for so long. And hope she could get the words out before one of her brothers killed him.

Two

Jeff left his borrowed car in the parking lot of the Shore Breakers hotel and walked the five blocks to Kelly's house. In this tiny beachside town, most of the residential streets were one-way and it was almost impossible to find a parking spot. And besides, it felt good to walk down quiet streets without having to worry about watching his back. He smiled to himself as he realized not for the first time that going out on those dangerous missions to every far-flung corner of the world never failed to make him appreciate the simple freedom of taking an afternoon stroll.

A car horn honked, the driver shouted and Jeff chuckled, preferring the everyday noises to that of gunfire pinging over his head. But even as that thought rushed through his mind, he pushed it on and out. Now wasn't the time to be thinking of the job. For the next month, all he wanted to think about was Kelly.

He'd been looking forward to this too much to spoil it now.

A cool breeze scuttled down the length of the narrow street and carried the scent of the ocean along with it. Jeff walked with the wind and felt it pushing him along, though he didn't need any encouragement.

Hell, he'd checked into his hotel room, dumped his bag on the bed and left, headed for Kelly's house. He didn't really need the hotel room, of course. He could have stayed on base. But when he was on leave, Jeff liked to get completely away from the job. He had a lot of unused pay stored up and besides, after eighteen months of roughing it in some *very* uncomfortable spots, he figured he'd earned a few luxuries. Like that giant Jacuzzi tub in the bathroom.

He smiled to himself and quickened his step a bit. Oh, yeah, he wanted to get Kelly into that oversize tub, turn up the heat—on the water, as well as Kelly—and do a little experimenting beneath the pulse of those jets.

His body stiffened instantly. Man. He rolled his shoulders and shook his head. Better watch the direction of his thoughts, or he wouldn't be able to walk. But it seemed the closer he got to Kelly's place, the more difficult it was to think of anything but her. Of putting his hands on her, feeling the brush of her breath on his face.

And that just naturally made his body sit up and take notice.

A whoop of laughter shattered his thoughts as a group of kids on skateboards and scooters raced by. Their voices hung in the clear air like pictures of innocence. Hell, Jeff didn't even remember being that young. That carefree. He pulled one hand from his pocket and scraped it across his jaw.

He'd gone from his last foster home directly into the Corps and had never looked back. Hadn't seemed to be much point in remembering the past. It hadn't been much fun living it, so why the hell would he want to waste time on memory lane?

Jeff glanced over his shoulder to make sure the street was clear, then loped across the narrow road, easing his way between two parked cars. The houses here were crouched together on skinny lots with postage-stamp-sized yards. But he supposed living less than a block from the beach was compensation enough. Most of the places were at least fifty years old, though some had been remodeled recently, going up two, sometimes three stories. Kids and dogs littered the street, the whole place looked like a fifties movie set and ordinarily it was exactly the kind of place Jeff would have avoided like the plague.

"That's a hell of a note," he muttered, smiling. "When a man feels more comfortable on a battlefield than in a neighborhood."

Still, seeing Kelly again would make it all worth it. If she was home. If she was still interested. If she even wanted to see him. "A whole lot of ifs in there," he told himself, and locked his gaze on the house just ahead. Kelly's place.

It looked like a miniature fairy-tale cottage. Complete with rounded turret. She'd told him her late grandmother had left it to her, but Jeff couldn't imagine anyone but Kelly living in it. It suited her, from the neatly trimmed hedges and flowers to the slate-gray tiles on the roof.

And now that he was here, he wasn't going to waste another minute admiring the damn house.

Lifting the latch on the gate in the pale yellow picket fence, he pushed it open, smiling again at the familiar creak. He slid a quick glance at the driveway, noting the navy-blue Explorer. Did she have visitors, or had she bought a new car while he was gone? Hell. Maybe he shouldn't have just left a message on her answering machine saying when he was coming over. Maybe he should have actually *talked* to her. For all he knew, she didn't have any interest at all in seeing him.

But it was too late now, he thought. If she was busy, he'd leave. And as he recalled, she didn't have any trouble speaking her mind, so if she didn't want to see him, she'd say so. But he'd waited too long to head back to the hotel now without even a glimpse of her. And if her visitor was a new boyfriend? Hell. He'd face that bridge if he came to it.

Decision made, he moved up the walk, took the two short steps to the porch and reached for the dragon's-head knocker on the heavy oak door. Lifting it, he smacked it twice on the pewter plate, then stood back smiling and waited.

When the door opened, his grin faded. He'd been expecting—hoping—to see a short redhead smiling up at him.

Instead, a Marine with dark brown hair and narrowed green eyes glared at him. "You Jeff Hunter?" he asked.

Instinctively, Jeff went on full alert. His own

gaze narrowed in return. Okay, so this little reunion wasn't starting out just the way he'd planned. He tried to see past the man into the house, but he was taking up the whole damn doorway.

"Who are you?" he asked.

The Marine stiffened. "I'm asking the questions here. You Jeff Hunter?"

"Yeah," he said, "what's th—?"

The big man moved so fast, Jeff didn't have a chance to react. Before he could get out of the way, a fist plowed into his face, snapping his head back and filling his mouth with the coppery taste of blood. Pain exploded inside his head and his ears rang with it.

Damn, it had been years since he'd been blindsided like that. And generally, when he was punched, he had *some* idea *why*.

"I've been waiting to meet you," the guy said, and stepped out of the house, swinging that hamlike fist again. This time, though, Jeff was braced and ready. Head still pounding, he ducked under the blow and came up fighting.

His fist slammed into the other man's belly. "Who the hell are you?" he demanded even as he threw another punch after the first.

No answer. Just a forearm around Jeff's neck and a quick, flying trip to the tidy front lawn.

He rolled and came up on the balls of his feet, crouched and prepared for attack or defense. This was what he'd been trained for, after all. But he usually liked to know just who the hell he was fighting.

And somehow, it didn't sit right, pounding on a fellow Marine. But he didn't have much choice when the other man charged him, head down and bellowing like a bull. He got in a good shot and Jeff hit the ground. "That's it. Marine or not, you're goin' down," he promised as he jumped to his feet.

Their bodies crashed together with a thud, and as a series of punches landed on his jaw, stomach and chin, Jeff sucked in the pain, buried it as he'd been taught and gave more than he took. He swung a hardened fist at the big man's face and felt the sting of satisfaction ripple up his arm when it smacked the guy's head back.

"Had enough?"

"Not nearly," the other man answered.

Absently, Jeff noted the sound of birds and the far-off roar of a lawn mower. Unreal, he thought. This shouldn't be happening. He hadn't come here as a warrior, but as a lover.

"Who are you and where's Kelly?"

"Kelly's none of your business."

"I say she is," Jeff snapped, and threw a short, sharp jab at the man's chin.

"You're wrong," the man shouted, and landed a good shot to Jeff's jaw.

They circled each other warily and when he saw an opening, Jeff made a move to end this little battle. He threw a flying tackle his old high-school football coach would have been proud of. He took the man down and when he was flat on his back, Jeff grabbed hold of the neck of his uniform blouse, bunched it in his fist and lifted the other one menacingly, just inches from the man's nose.

"Okay," he said, dragging air into heaving lungs, "you want to tell me what we're fighting about?"

"You son of a bitch," the man muttered. "The fact that you don't even know is reason enough to keep fighting." He reached for Jeff's throat.

"Are you nuts?" A familiar female voice shouted from the porch, cutting the man off mid-speech, and Jeff swung his head around to look at Kelly.

His opponent used the distraction to plant one more solid punch to Jeff's jaw. Stars flashed in front of his eyes.

"Blast it, Kevin!" she called, racing down off the porch and across the lawn. She stood over them, hands at her hips, glaring at the man on the ground. "Stop hitting him. I warned you...no fighting."

Jeff wiggled his jaw back and forth a couple of times, ran his tongue around the inside of his mouth checking for loose teeth and, thankfully, found none. Then he turned a feral smile on the man still glaring at him. "I owe you for that one."

"Anytime," he countered, breathing hard as Jeff released him.

What the hell was going on around here, anyway? Why was a fellow Marine ready to pound his face in when as far as Jeff knew, they'd never met before?

"I don't believe this," Kelly muttered, glancing up and down the street, obviously looking to see if any of her neighbors had witnessed the brawl.

Pain flickered through his body in a series of stings and aches, but despite it all, he felt his blood go thick and hot at the sight of her. Damn, but she looked good, Jeff thought and felt his body stir.

She wore a soft green skirt that fell to her ankles and swirled around her legs in the cool wind. Her long-sleeved yellow blouse clung to her upper body, outlining her small, perfect breasts and made

Jeff's hands itch to touch them. Long auburn curls flew into a wild dance around her head, and her green eyes sparkled with what looked like pure temper. Yep, he thought, wincing with a new twinge of pain. Damn good.

"Hi, Kelly," he said, and felt the full impact of her fury when she shifted her gaze to him.

"'Hi Kelly'?" she repeated. "That's all you have to say? I find you brawling in my front yard with Kevin, and all you say is 'hi'?"

"Go inside, Kelly," the other man said. "This is between him and me."

She kicked him, then winced as her bare toes connected with his hipbone. "For heaven's sake, Kevin," she snapped. "Stop acting like the puritan father in an old movie."

"Damn it, Kelly..."

"I told you I wanted to talk to Jeff alone."

"Just who the hell are you, anyway?" Jeff interrupted, glaring at the man he'd just been pounding into the ground.

"Kevin Rogan. I'm Kelly's brother."

Brother. Well, that was good news, anyway. Sort of. Probably wasn't the best way to impress a woman you hadn't seen in a year and a half—beating up on her brother. But on the other hand, at least he wasn't a boyfriend.

Jeff pushed himself to his feet and waited while Kevin did the same. Tension still rippled in the air between them, and Jeff sensed the other man's eagerness to continue the fight. Fine with him, he thought, already taking a step toward him. Then, before either of them could start up again, Kelly stepped between them, placing one hand on each of their chests.

"Obviously, an overdose of testosterone. Play nice or leave," she said, looking from one to the other of them.

"Fine," Kevin said flatly. "But I'm not leaving."

"Neither am I," Jeff told him. "I just got here."

"Yeah," Kevin said with a derisive snort, "but you've been here before, haven't you?"

"What's that supposed to mean?"

"You bastard, if you'd—"

"Kevin…" Kelly interrupted her brother with one word and a long warning look.

Then, turning her back on him, she smiled at Jeff. "It's good to see you."

Kevin snorted again.

"Got a cold?" Jeff asked, then ignored the man and reached out to touch Kelly's hair, blowing wild and gorgeous in the breeze. He had to see if it was as soft and silky as he remembered.

It was.

"Good to see you, too," he said, knowing it for the understatement of the century. It was worth a few bruises and what felt like a cracked rib or two to see her smile. Damn, but he'd missed her.

"You going to introduce us, sis?" Another male voice spoke up, and Jeff glanced at the porch. Lined up like a wall of muscle with bad attitudes, three men—identical men—stood with arms crossed over wide chests. And each one of them wore a scowl fierce enough to fry bacon.

Specifically, Jeff guessed, *his* bacon. *What* was going on around here?

"More brothers?" Jeff muttered, more to himself than to Kelly.

"Yes, but the triplets are the last of them. Four older brothers." She blew out a breath that ruffled the loose curls lying across her forehead. "Lucky me."

Yeah, Jeff thought, glancing from the triplets to Kevin, still glowering at him from the lawn. He was starting to feel real lucky himself.

She lifted one hand and with a sigh, pointed to each of the three in turn. "Jeff, this is Keith, Kieran and Kincaid."

If anything, their scowls got blacker. Interesting, Jeff thought, wishing that he had Deke, J.T. and

Travis backing him up. He was badly outnumbered.

"They Marines, too?" he asked.

"No, just Kevin. Keith's a policeman, Kieran's a contractor and Kincaid's a—" She paused, cocked her head and looked at her last brother. "What would you call it? A spy?"

For the first time, Jeff saw a chink in the wall of muscle as Kincaid smiled at his sister. "FBI, Kelly. Hardly a spy."

She shrugged. "Well, whatever. So why don't you guys get lost while I talk to Jeff?"

"Not hardly," Kevin muttered, and walked past her, pausing just long enough to glare at Jeff again. Then he nodded to his brothers, and the four of them went into the house.

No doubt, Jeff thought, to lay an ambush for him. Man, what had he done to get all four men so damn mad? Hell, he hadn't even been in the country for the past year and a half!

"I tried to get rid of them," Kelly was saying, "but once they found out you were coming, they wouldn't budge."

"I don't care about them," Jeff said. "I'm here to see you. It's been a long time, Kelly."

"Yeah," she said, smiling up at him, "it really has."

"You look great," he told her, and for the first time in eighteen months, reached out and cupped her cheek in the palm of his hand. God, she felt good. Soft, warm and so damn smooth. Just the touch of her skin was enough to set off a back fire in his blood. And if she didn't have a platoon of brothers just a stone's throw away, he'd show her just how glad he was to see her. As it was, he'd have to wait or take on all four of them.

She pulled in a long shaky breath, telling him silently that she was just as affected as he was. A flush of heat filled her cheeks, and her eyes went that deep, smoky green that he remembered so clearly.

But there was something else. Something...*different* about her. She looked rounder. Softer. Hell, the plain truth was, she looked good enough to eat. And he was a hungry man.

"What?" she asked, tipping her head to one side and looking up at him.

"Hmm?"

"You're looking at me a little...strangely."

"I'm just trying to figure out what it is that's different about you."

"Different?"

"Not different bad, honey," he said, pulling her close enough to kiss. "Just...different."

Kelly flattened her palms on his chest and leaned toward him. A soft ocean wind slipped past them and lifted her hair off her neck. He felt the warmth of her hands clean through to his bones and for the first time in too damn long, he felt alive again.

The scent of her surrounded him, and he lost himself in it. So many nights, he'd dreamed about this moment. Having his hands on her again. Feeling the soft brush of her breath against his skin. Cupping her face in his palms, he stroked her cheeks with the pads of his thumbs and let his gaze move over her features. She was even more beautiful than he remembered.

She reached up and covered his hands with her own. "Jeff, I'm sorry about Kevin. He's just—"

He grinned down at her. With her right here beside him, he couldn't have cared less about a handful of brothers with bad attitudes.

"Kevin who?" he asked, and bent his head to claim the kiss he'd waited so long for. She leaned into him, lifting up onto her toes to meet that kiss and do a little taking of her own.

Softly at first, as if reminding himself of the taste of her, Jeff quickly gave into the thrumming need inside him and deepened the kiss. He parted her lips with his tongue and explored her mouth as his hands moved up and down her spine, pulling her harder, closer against him.

Kelly clung to him, and gave herself up to the wonder of having him back home. Alive. Safe. The magic of his touch shimmered throughout her body, and she told herself that she hadn't imagined it. It had been so long, she'd almost convinced herself that what she'd felt in Jeff's arms couldn't possibly have been real. Yet here he was, and once again her body was on fire and burning from the inside out.

The shriek of a child's laughter finally shattered the spell, though, and Kelly reluctantly pulled free of his arms. After all, what with the fight and now this kiss, they'd given her neighbors enough of a show for today.

Besides, there were still a few things that had to be said.

"Jeff..."

"Yeah?" His hand slipped from her cheek to her neck, and his thumb rested on the pulse point at the base of her throat.

"Come on in the house," she said, and reached up to take his hand in hers.

He laughed shortly. "With that bunch? Am I allowed to fight back?"

She grinned at him. "Don't worry about them.

I've been dealing with them for years. Their barks are worse than their bites."

Jeff rubbed his jaw. "Honey, if that's his bark, I don't want to *see* his bite."

"Hey," she countered, "are you saying a Recon Marine isn't tough enough to handle three civilians and a Gunnery Sergeant?"

"If that's a challenge, honey," he said in a low growl, "consider it taken."

Three

The inside of the house was just as he remembered it. He'd always thought it looked a bit like a child's playhouse might. The rooms were small, cozy. Fresh flowers dotted every table, and brightly colored pillows were stacked on all of the chairs. It was cool, welcoming, with the faint scent of lavender flavoring the still air. Pale blue walls gave the impression of a soft summer day, and the overstuffed furniture invited people to settle in and stay for a while. And there was nothing he would've liked more.

However, the four huge brothers glowering at

him from across the room took the edge off his homecoming.

He had no idea what he'd done to deserve all the hostility, but he was damned if he'd back off. Jeff's spine stiffened and he lifted his already bruised chin. His body still humming from that kiss, he was prepared to face down whomever he had to to get Kelly to himself.

Unconsciously, he mirrored the brothers' stance. Arms crossed, legs braced wide apart and a defiant glint in his eyes. One at a time or all four at once…Jeff was ready for them.

"Kelly," Kevin said, "I think we should—"

Jeff's gaze shifted to Kevin and he felt a brief spurt of satisfaction at the other man's split lip and already blackening eye. On the couch in front of him was a Smokey Bear hat, and Jeff knew that Kelly's older brother was a drill instructor. He should have guessed when he heard the man talk earlier. His voice was rough from too much shouting, and he was talking to his sister as if he were giving orders to a boot recruit.

And from what Jeff remembered of Kelly's temperament, her reaction should be worth watching.

He was right.

"Kevin," Kelly spoke up, interrupting him, "I think you've done *enough* for one day."

"Hey, this wasn't Kevin's fault," one of the triplets said.

"Really?" she asked, turning on him like a snake. "Who punched whom?"

The big guy actually backed up a step, and Jeff hid a smile. Man, it was good to watch her in action. For such a small thing, she had enough fire in her for three women. And seeing her set loose that temper on her overbearing brothers was damn entertaining.

However, he wasn't going to stand there and keep quiet while she defended him against her own family.

"Whatever your problem is with me," he said, staring straight into Kevin's flat gaze, "I'd be happy to settle it with you."

The other man tensed. "Anytime, Gunnery Sergeant."

"Fine," Jeff muttered, already gearing up to finish what had been started outside. "Let's go."

"Nobody's going anywhere," Kelly snapped, looking from Jeff to her oldest brother.

"Kelly," Kevin spoke up again in that drill instructor growl of his. "We've been waiting to talk to him for a long time."

"So have I," she retorted.

"Well, I'm standing right here," Jeff said, looking from Kevin to Kelly and back again. They were all so busy talking around him and about him, no one was talking *to* him, and a tiny thread of warning unraveled inside him. Something was definitely up, and he wanted to know just what it was. "How about somebody tells me what's going on around here?"

Kelly turned toward him, and for the first time he noticed a slight tension etched into her features. She looked worried. But about what?

Kevin opened his mouth again, but Kelly gave him a look that could have toasted a lesser man and he scowled, but kept quiet.

"This isn't going at all how I planned it," she said, turning back to Jeff, her wide eyes focused on him as if he were the only man there. "I want you to know that. I tried to get rid of them earlier, but they just wouldn't move."

Jeff ignored the brothers, which wasn't easy since they took up so much space in the small room. But if she could do it, he sure as hell could. Keeping his gaze locked on her, he said simply, "Forget them, Kelly. Just talk to me."

She inhaled sharply and blew the air out in a rush, ruffling the loose curls on her forehead. How many times had he thought of that little gesture of hers? How many nights had he dreamed of being right here…in this house…with her? Well, here he was, but so far the reality was nothing like his imagination.

"You're right," she said, nodding. "This is between you and me, no matter what they think." She gave her brothers a warning look, then stepped forward, took Jeff's hand and led him into the hall toward the two tiny bedrooms.

He felt the combined gazes of those brothers boring a hole into his back, but he did his best to ignore it. The last time he'd walked down this hall, he remembered, Kelly had been in his arms, nestled against his chest. If he tried, he could almost feel the beat of her heart against his again. Enjoying the memory, he let it unfold, recalling how he'd carried her into her bedroom, laid her down atop the bed and then fell into her welcoming arms.

It had been their last night together. A night that had lasted until morning. A night that had been burned into his brain with such clarity that even now, with her brothers hot on his heels, he felt a rush of desire so strong it nearly swamped him. But, he reminded himself, that was then and this was now.

A tinkle of music drifted toward him, along with a scent that he really didn't recognize. It was soft and pleasant and faintly familiar, though he couldn't place it. Behind him, he heard the heavy footsteps of the four men who were following after them and Jeff wished again he had either a weapon or his team with him.

But Kelly's fingers were warm on his, and rather than waste any more time thinking about her brothers, he concentrated instead on the woman in front of him. His gaze dropped to the sway of her hips as she walked, and another sharp, sweet jolt of desire rocked him. Whatever was between them was damn strong, he thought. That he could respond to the mere fact of her presence while surrounded by her hostile family was proof enough of that.

Time was wasting, he thought, wanting only to see whatever it was she had to show him, then get on with the reunion. That one kiss they'd shared had only whetted his appetite, and he knew he wouldn't be satisfied until he was buried inside her body, feeling the warmth of her ease back all the darkness within him. She was the only woman who'd ever been able to do that, he thought. It was only with Kelly that he'd been able to find the kind of peace that most people took for granted.

Jeff wasn't a man to plan on forever. He'd learned long ago to count on nothing but now. Today. Planning for tomorrows that might not come was useless. But for however long this lasted, he wanted to cherish the time with Kelly. Revel in all he found with her so that when it was over, he'd be able to dredge up the memories and recall a time, however brief, when he wasn't alone.

She glanced over her shoulder and gave him a smile that lit up his insides like a firefight at midnight. And every thought but one fled from his mind. All he wanted, all he needed, was her. The feel of her. The taste of her. His insides shook with the need to touch her. So, he told himself, let's get this show on the road, and then send those brothers of hers packing.

Then she opened a closed door and pulled him into a pale yellow room where his sexual fancies died a quick death.

He noticed the crib first. Something clutched tight in his chest. But before he had time to wonder why in the hell Kelly had a crib in her house, the baby inside that crib grabbed hold of the bars with two tiny fists and pulled itself to its feet. There it stood, dark hair, blue eyes, wide grin and drool running from the corner of its mouth. It looked at them all, bounced a couple of times, then giggled and fell backward onto the mattress.

His mouth dried up. He shot a look at Kelly. "What?" Words failed him. What the hell was he supposed to say? She was a *mother?* Was she married, too? His gaze flicked down to her bare ring finger, and knew he should have felt relieved. But there were still too many unanswered questions for relief to come into this yet. If she had a baby, where was the father? And just what kind of reaction was she expecting from him? Couldn't she have prepared him just a little for this?

"Jeff," she said, her voice soft, intimate, "meet Emily."

"Emily," he repeated, and silently congratulated himself on getting his own voice to work. A knot of some unidentifiable emotion lodged in his throat, and Jeff choked it down. There was more coming. He knew it. He could feel it. And he braced himself for it.

And even when he was braced, her next words rocked his world right out from under him.

"Your daughter," Kelly added, and the final blow hit him hard to the chest. Air rushed out of his lungs, and he wasn't at all sure he'd be able to pull more in. All right, this he hadn't expected. But it sure as hell explained her brothers' attitudes toward him.

If this baby really was his, the four of them probably wanted to murder him. And he couldn't even find it in him to blame them.

A curl of foreboding settled in the pit of Jeff's

stomach. His baby! Good God, Jeff thought wildly. He couldn't be a *father*. He was a *Marine*. And father to a girl? What the hell did he know about girls—except, of course, for the grown-up version? No. There had to be a mistake.

"My daughter?" he repeated, even knowing that he was beginning to sound like an echo.

"Damn right, your daughter," Kevin said from the doorway. "And what are you going to do about it?"

Okay, understanding the anger was one thing; putting up with it was another. Jeff turned on him. "Well, hell, why don't you give me more than ten seconds to get used to the idea, huh?"

"What's to get used to," the other man argued. "You have a child. Unless you're going to try to deny her."

"Damn it, Kevin," Kelly said, and rushed at her mountain of a brother. Planting both hands on his broad chest, she shoved for all she was worth and actually succeeded in backing him up a step or two before he dug in his heels and held his ground.

"This is family business," one of the other brothers said, keeping his voice carefully neutral. "We have the right to hear what he has to say."

When she would have argued that point, Jeff

said, "He has a point. They do have the right to talk to me about this."

Surprise flashed across Kevin's face, but he nodded, clearly pleased. Until Jeff continued.

"But first, Kelly and I are going to talk. Alone."

"Exactly," she said, and waved both hands at her brothers, herding them toward the door. "You guys get lost so Jeff and I can settle this between us."

One of the triplets spoke up then. "Fine. We'll go. But this isn't over."

Now, *that,* Jeff thought, was putting it mildly. But as he turned back to face the crib, he pushed Kelly's brothers out of his mind and tried to focus on the shift his life had just taken.

He had a daughter.

It never occurred to him to doubt Kelly's word on this. She wasn't the kind of woman to lie about something this huge. If she said he was the father, then that's just what he was.

But how had this happened?

When he and Kelly were together, they'd been careful. They'd used protection. Hell, he'd gone through enough condoms in that two-week period to justify buying stock in the company. So how did they manage to create a baby? This kind of thing didn't happen to responsible adults. Surprise babies happened to high-school kids with more hormones than sense.

Swiveling his head, he stared hard at Kelly for a long moment, looking for some sign that she was somehow kidding. Maybe she was baby-sitting, a small, hopeful voice inside him said, completely discounting the fact that the room was a magazine version of a perfect nursery. One last chance here, he told himself. It was a joke. A bad one. But there was no laughter in her eyes. Only the same tension he'd noted earlier.

So much for a last-minute reprieve.

The baby gurgled again, and Jeff forced leaden feet to carry him farther into the room. Pale yellow walls glimmered in the afternoon sunshine streaming through the windows. Teddy bears and baby dolls littered the floor, and a mobile of sea horses dangled over the crib, dancing weirdly to the tinny tune he'd heard earlier.

Dread crashed down around him. A baby. In Kelly's house. A baby with black hair and blue eyes. A baby that looked—except for the lack of a five-o'clock shadow—too much like Jeff for comfort.

He stood in front of the crib, gripped the top rail in two tight fists and stared down at the baby through eyes glazed with confusion and just a hint of panic. The tiny girl kicked both legs, lifted her arms toward him and gave him a smile that both terrified and touched him more deeply than he would have thought possible.

A child.

He had a child.

God help the poor little thing.

With her brothers gone, Kelly drew her first easy breath all evening. It was hard enough telling Jeff about the baby without the added factor of four men ready and willing to beat him into the ground.

But now that it was just her and Jeff, a wave of discomfort rippled through her. This was so much more difficult than she'd thought it would be. He looked, she thought, like a man who'd been hit over the head with a two-by-four. And she couldn't blame him.

"I'm sorry this is such a shock," she said, and winced at the inadequacy of the words.

"Shock?" he muttered, shaking his head. "Good word for this."

"I would have told you sooner," Kelly went on, walking across the room to stand beside him, "but I had no way to get in touch with you."

She looked down at her daughter and felt her heart melt as it always did with one look at Emily.

Amazing how such a tiny person could engender such great amounts of love.

From the moment she'd discovered she was pregnant, Kelly had loved her child with a fierceness she hadn't thought she was capable of. And she'd wanted to tell Jeff about the baby. But he'd told her in the beginning of their relationship that he was in the Marine Force Recon. Always on the move. Always involved in some covert action, stealing in and out of hostile situations.

She had every postcard he'd sent her over the past year and a half. But there'd been no return address. No way to reach him. And when she'd contacted the base, trying to get in touch with him, she'd been told simply that he was in the field.

"But I called you—" he said, glancing at her briefly. "six months ago, I telephoned you from Guam."

"A five-minute phone call, Jeff," she said in her own defense. "Five minutes on a static-filled line."

She remembered that phone call all too clearly. The sound of his voice, so faraway, so faint. The bursts of white noise that slashed at their tenuous link. She'd wanted to tell him so badly. Wanted him to know about Emily. But how could she have done that to him when he was so far away, going into who knew what kind of danger?

She hadn't wanted to distract him. Hadn't wanted to be the cause of his getting hurt or killed on some mission or other because his mind was on something other than the job.

His hands tightened on the crib rail until his knuckles went white. "How long does it take to say, 'We have a baby girl'?"

A flush of anger swept through her. "Longer than five minutes," she said. "I couldn't just announce Emily's existence and then not be able to talk to you about it."

"Damn it, Kelly, I had the right to know."

"Yeah, you did. But how was I supposed to track you down to tell you?"

He pulled in a long, deep breath and slanted her a look. "Okay, fine. Maybe there was no way to tell me before. But tell me now. How did this happen?"

She drew her head back and looked at him. "How? For heaven's sake Jeff, we made love nearly every day for two solid weeks."

"And used condoms," he pointed out.

"Apparently, one of them didn't work."

"Didn't work?" he demanded. "How could they not work? That's their only job!"

Kelly laughed shortly. Hadn't she asked herself those very questions when she did that first pregnancy test? But asking how wasn't going to solve a thing now. It was a little late to worry about the inadequacies of condoms.

"Yeah, well," she said softly as she smiled down at her daughter, "that's not really important now, is it?"

He sighed and followed her gaze back to the child staring up at them with wide blue eyes. "I guess not. But damn, Kelly. This wasn't exactly the kind of reunion I was expecting."

"I know," she said, and reached out to lay one hand atop his.

A short, choked laugh shot from his throat. "Well, at least I know why your brother tried to tear my head off."

He didn't know the half of it. Since telling her brothers that she was pregnant, all four of them had been just itching to get their hands on the man responsible.

"I'm sorry about Kevin," she said, "but my brothers have always tried to protect me—even when I didn't want them to."

"Can't blame 'em," Jeff said, and reached out to touch her cheek before letting his hand fall to his side. "If I were in their shoes, I'd be pretty damn mad at me, too."

"As much as I love them," Kelly told him, "it doesn't matter what they say in the end. Emily is *our* daughter. *We* decide what to do and where to go from here."

"You're right," Jeff said, nodding and straightening up to full attention. "And where we go from here is to the closest justice of the peace we can find."

"Huh?"

"We're getting married."

Four

And that was a word he'd never thought to use in a sentence.

Married.

He scraped one hand across his jaw and looked down into Kelly's sea-green eyes. Jeff had never once in his entire life considered the idea of marriage. Hell, why should he? He'd spend most of his growing-up years in a too-crowded county home. And when he'd finally been placed in a foster home, he'd seen up close and personal just how miserable a bad marriage could be on everyone.

He'd escaped that home as soon as he turned

eighteen and enlisted in the Corps. There, he'd found his niche in the world. The one place he belonged. The notion of honor and duty had struck a chord with him, giving Jeff the firm footing he'd always craved. He'd excelled in marksmanship and handling explosives, eventually earning himself a spot in Recon Forces, the Marine Corps's answer to the Navy SEALs—only better. It was an important job and a dangerous life. One that didn't lend itself to home-and-hearth type relationships. Which had never bothered him any, since until Kelly he'd never really had anyone to care about.

And as to being a father? Well, that went along with marriage in his mind. He'd been the unwanted child of an unwed mother and wasn't about to foist that burden on some unsuspecting kid of his own.

Nope. Emily was his daughter. And he was going to do right by her.

"We are *not* getting married," Kelly told him with a shake of her head.

"Oh, yes, we are," Jeff told her. "As soon as I can arrange it."

"Listen, Jeff," she said.

"No," he interrupted her quickly. He knew what his duty was here. He'd left Kelly holding the proverbial bag eighteen months ago. Okay, sure, he hadn't known about it. But now that he did, he was going to make up for not being around when she'd needed him.

He'd thought of Kelly so often during the past year and a half. Every dream was filled with her image. Every spare moment, his thoughts turned to her. He'd mailed postcards from every port, enjoying for the first time actually having someone at home to write to. It hadn't mattered that there'd been no way to receive mail from her. It had been enough just knowing she was there. At home. Safe. He'd enjoyed the thought that she might actually *miss* him. And how many times had he wondered if she thought of him as much as he had her?

Well, now he knew that she couldn't have helped thinking of him. She had a living, breathing reminder of him right there with her, twenty-four hours a day.

And something inside him was so damn grateful that she hadn't ended the pregnancy. That she hadn't given his child away. Emotion coiled in his gut, and he fought it down. The only way to win a battle was to stay clearheaded, and judging by the look in Kelly's eyes, they were about to go to war.

"Jeff, getting married isn't the answer here."

"What is?" he asked, and from the corner of his eye, he saw little Emily pulling herself up in the crib again. Strong, he thought. And healthy. And damn pretty, he told himself.

Kelly opened her mouth, then snapped it closed again. Lifting both hands high, she let them fall back to her sides and then shrugged. "I don't even know if there *is* an answer. I just wanted you to know about Emily. I want you to be a part of her life, if you want to."

"If I *want* to?" he asked. Could she really believe that he'd turn and run when confronted with a child he'd created? Did she think so little of him?

"Wrong choice of words," she said, lifting one hand, palm out in a peaceful gesture. "Of course you want to. All I meant was that Emily deserves to know her father."

Yeah, he thought. She did. But what would she think of a man who didn't have the slightest idea of just *how* to be the father she deserved? Would he let her down? Would he not be good enough?

The baby slapped at his hands, still curled around the top rail of the crib. Jeff's gaze shifted to the little girl, and he found himself staring into eyes so much like his own, it was eerie. An unseen fist tightened around his heart and squeezed until the sensation was damn near painful.

Then Emily grabbed hold of a fistful of his shirt and lifted one small foot as though trying to climb the bars enclosing her. She wanted up and she wanted *him* to lift her. Just why that hit him so hard was a mystery to Jeff, but giving in to the child and his own temptation to hold her, he cupped his hands beneath her arms and picked her up. Her feet bounced and kicked and she threw herself at him, trusting him to hold on to her. To keep her safe.

And as easily as that, she fell into his heart. And that heart, the one he'd thought was so insulated against love, stirred with feelings so deep and so thick, he wasn't sure what to do about them. Just as he didn't have a clue what to do about Kelly.

Granted, his proposal wasn't the most romantic one in the world. But hey, he'd never done this before.

One arm cradling her well-padded behind, Jeff kept his free hand on Emily's back to make sure she wouldn't take a dive backward. And while he held her, inhaled the now recognizable scent of baby powder, he turned to look at Kelly again.

Late-afternoon sunlight streamed through the window and set the fiery colors of her hair aflame. A half smile curved her lips, and the unmistakable sheen of tears clouded her eyes as she looked at him with their daughter. "She likes you already."

He hoped so. "Kelly..."

She shook her head before he could get started. "Don't start the marriage thing again, Jeff. Please."

"Did you really think I *wouldn't* want to get married?"

She laughed shortly and scooped a handful of her hair back from her forehead. "I didn't know what to think. Jeff, we hardly knew each other."

He didn't believe that. In the two weeks he'd spent with Kelly, he'd felt closer to her than he had to anyone else in his life. And he knew she'd felt the same connection. What other reason was there for two perfect strangers to meet and then spend every waking minute together?

Okay, sure, there was the physical side of it. The sex had been amazing. But there was more there than just the lovemaking. They'd talked, and taken long walks on the beach. She'd told him about her job as a kindergarten teacher, and he'd told her all about the Corps and what it meant to him to belong. Maybe they hadn't learned everything about each other then—he certainly didn't remember hearing about four brothers—but it hadn't been a casual fling. He'd had enough of those to know the difference.

"You knew, Kelly," he said softly, daring her to deny it. "You knew I'd want to marry you."

* * *

She sighed heavily and admitted, "Yes. I guess I did." After all, her brother Kevin was a Marine, and that was exactly what he would have done in this position. And precisely what he'd insisted all along that Jeff do as soon as he returned. The Marines must drill honor and duty into these guys day and night, she told herself.

But even as that thought entered her mind, she discounted it. It wasn't the Corps talking here. It was Jeff. She'd known from the first moment she met him that he was a decent, responsible man. It was only natural that he would propose. Just as natural as it was for her to refuse him.

"Then what's the problem?" Jeff asked.

"The problem," she said, tipping her head back so she could meet his gaze squarely, "is that a baby is *not* reason enough to get married."

He snorted a choked-off laugh. "I don't know why not."

"Because we'd be getting married for all the wrong reasons."

"To protect Emily is the wrong reason?"

"Of course not," she snapped, and then lowered her voice when the baby's eyes went wide and confused. "But we don't have to be married to protect our daughter."

"To protect her from *some* things we do."

"Like?"

He ground his teeth together for a long minute, then blurted, "Like to keep her from being called a bastard, for instance."

Kelly drew her head back and stared at him. Was he serious? "For heaven's sake, Jeff. This isn't the fifties. There's no stigma attached to a child anymore."

He shifted his gaze from her to their daughter. "Maybe not to adults, but other kids know just how to hurt each other. And trust me when I tell you that sticks and stones aren't the only things that can hurt a child."

Old pain flashed across his features and was gone again so quickly, Kelly couldn't be sure she'd seen it at all. But listening to the sound of his voice convinced her that he'd had some experience with nasty children.

"We can love her enough that it won't matter to her," she said, laying one hand on his arm.

"It'll matter," Jeff said quietly. "She won't say so, but it'll matter."

Her heart ached for the boy he'd once been, but because he'd suffered didn't mean the same thing would happen to Emily. She would keep her daughter safe. She would go on providing a warm, loving home for her. And she didn't need a husband to do it.

All her life, Kelly had been surrounded by men trying to tell her what to do and how to do it. She'd learned young how to stand up for herself, how to withstand well-meant bullying, and she wasn't about to back up now. The one thing she *didn't* need in her life was one more male issuing orders.

"Then I'll just have to teach her to ignore them."

"Damn it, Kelly," he said, tearing his gaze from the baby still clutched tightly to his chest, "*we* made this baby. It's *our* responsibility to take care of her."

She sighed inwardly. It was a hard thing to fight against a man's sense of honor. But she wouldn't be the pill he had to swallow. The medicine he had to take. The bed he had to lie in simply because he'd made it.

"Jeff," she said, "you don't *owe* me anything. I'm perfectly capable of raising Emily on my own."

"I didn't say you weren't."

"I know, but you're not listening to me. I didn't want anything from you. I just wanted you to be able to know your daughter."

"Kelly..."

She shook her head, and hoped he would quit arguing. That he would accept her decision and let it be. But she had a feeling there was as much chance of that as seeing snow on an Easter Sunday at the beach.

A part of her wished things could be different. Those two weeks with Jeff had been almost...*magical*. She'd never felt such an instant *oneness* with anyone before. It was as if from the moment he'd plucked her unconscious from the ocean and breathed life back into her, they'd been bound together. He touched her in so many ways. Her heart ached when he left, and she'd looked back on every minute of their time together, wondering if she'd somehow imagined it all.

Until, of course, the stick turned blue and she'd discovered she was pregnant. Then it was all too real. Then she was left to wonder about Jeff, worrying about where he was, what he was doing— while at the same time dealing with her own changing life. And four irate brothers.

And now that Jeff was back, the magic between them was still there. She'd felt it the moment he'd kissed her out on the front lawn. But it wasn't just the two of them anymore. Now there was Emily to consider.

And how could she agree to marry Jeff, knowing

that he'd only proposed because of their daughter? She didn't want a husband who felt as though he'd been pushed into a marriage. Heck, she'd never really wanted a husband at all. She didn't need one more man in her life, even if it was the man who could set her body on fire with no more than a glance.

A quick flush of heat stole over her body, and in an effort to conceal it, she snatched the baby from Jeff's arms and held her tight. She ought to be ashamed, hiding behind her daughter. But at the moment, she was too desperate to argue the point.

"Emily deserves a mother *and* a father," he said, his gaze moving over his child's features as if he just couldn't look at her enough.

Kelly fought back a thread of temper. She'd give him a little leeway here. After all, he'd only just found out about Emily. "She *has* a mother and a father," she said, proud of her quiet self-control.

"Together, Kelly," he said, in a tone that reminded her far too much of her brothers when they were on a "we-know-best" kick.

Instinctively, Kelly's spine went ramrod straight.

"She deserves to have two parents. Together." Jeff threw his hands wide. "Hell, *every* kid deserves that!"

That last sentence came a little loud for Emily's

tastes, and the little girl screwed up her face and let out a wail that had Jeff's face blanching.

"What is it?" he asked. "What's wrong with her?"

"What's wrong," Kelly snapped, feeling the last of her patience unravel, "is that her *father* shouted and scared her."

Shame swept across his features, and he ducked his head and winced when Emily kept crying. "I didn't mean to scare her."

"I know that," Kelly said. "She, unfortunately, doesn't."

Jiggling the baby in her arms, she cooed and whispered to her, inhaling the sweet, soft scent that was Emily's alone. And as the baby quieted again, Kelly felt her heart swell to bursting with love for this tiny person who was so much a part of her world now, she couldn't imagine life without her. Looking up at Jeff, she saw regret shining in his eyes and took pity on him.

"It's okay, Jeff. She's fine."

"She's got a great set of lungs," he muttered, and winced again when the baby turned a tear-stained face toward him. He reached out one hand to her, but before he could touch her, he curled his fingers into a tight fist and let his hand drop to his side. "Look, Kelly," he said, "maybe I said this all wrong. And I know that wasn't the most romantic proposal in the world. But I just want to do the right thing here.''

"I know that, Jeff," she said. "I really do. But getting married just isn't it."

Kelly noticed his jaw muscle twitch and she knew she hadn't heard the last of this conversation. He had thirty days' leave, and knowing Jeff, he would be there every day of it. He would slide back into her life. Into Emily's life.

And she didn't know if she could stand that, knowing that he'd only be leaving again.

Five

Back at his hotel room…*alone,* Jeff sat in the dark staring out at the moonlit ocean five floors below him. From a distance, he heard voices drifting in the night air and knew that other couples had found each other in the darkness. And he felt more isolated than he ever had before.

Sighing to himself, Jeff eased down into one of the twin chairs positioned on the narrow balcony, propped his feet on the rail in front of him and stared out at the ocean. Moonlight glimmered on the water's surface, laying down a silvery path toward eternity. Stars were sprinkled across the black sky, and a soft, cold wind blew in off the ocean, tugging at the collar of his shirt. A chill crawled down his spine, but he shook it off, too intent on his thoughts to worry about the cold.

He'd left Kelly just an hour ago, but she hadn't been off his mind for an instant. Of course, her image in his brain now shared space with his daughter's tiny face.

His daughter.

Jeff reached up and scraped one hand across his face as if he rubbed hard enough, he could wipe away the confusion...the shock that still reverberated throughout his body. But it wouldn't be that easy. Hell, nothing would be easy ever again.

His entire world had shifted, moved into a brand-new sphere, and he didn't have a clue what to do about it. Reaching for the bottle of beer sitting on the table beside him, Jeff took a long drink, then set it down again. All of his life, he'd avoided committing to anyone or anything besides the Corps.

Not that he had anything against commitment— it was just that he'd never really thought of himself as the family type. What did he know about families? Nothing, that's what. And hell, little girls?

He reached for his beer again, even knowing that it wouldn't do any good. What he needed was a plan. Some idea of what to do next. Some *help*. But there was no help to be had. He was on his own. As he had been most of his life.

That thought floated to the surface of his mind, and he pushed it aside. No time for regrets. This was a time for action. But what kind of action? He'd already proposed and been turned down flat. Hell, he'd argued till he was blue in the face, but Kelly, stubborn woman that she was, hadn't given an inch. Ordinarily, he would have enjoyed that. He liked a strong woman. One who could stand on her own two feet. But damn it. Not *now*.

"Back to a plan," he muttered, not thinking twice about talking to himself. He usually worked out his problems best when speaking them aloud. Somehow, it seemed easier that way. "So what I need here is a battle strategy. This is no different than sneaking into enemy territory. I've got to reach my objective and get back out before the enemy knows what's up." Unfortunately, the enemy in this case was Kelly.

She was standing firm against him and what he knew was the right thing to do. And he had to find a way around her defenses.

He knew how he'd *like* to get around them, and as images chased each other through his mind, his body went hard and his blood boiled in his veins.

Damn, he wanted to touch her. Wanted to feel her soft, smooth skin next to his. "Okay," he told himself firmly, "that's not going to get you anywhere." Except right where he wanted to be. Inside her.

Jeff yanked his feet off the rail and stood up, a sudden, restless energy pulsing through him, demanding action. Maybe a run on the beach, he thought, glancing down at the nearly deserted stretch of sand. He had to move. To get his blood pumping. And since what he wanted to do was denied him…at least for tonight, a fast five-mile run would have to do.

Turning around, he marched into the hotel room, stalked across the mini-living room of the small suite and entered the bedroom. He tugged his T-shirt off, then bent to take off his boots. As he pulled off his socks and undid the top button on the fly of his jeans, a knock on the door stopped him.

Frowning, Jeff moved soundlessly across the carpet, back through the living room to the small entryway. He turned the knob, yanked the door open and stared, openmouthed at Kelly.

Her mouth went dry.

Good God, she thought, her gaze sweeping over

him quickly, thoroughly. She'd actually forgotten just what a hunk Jeff Hunter really was. His bare chest looked as though it had been sculpted by a master out of teakwood. Tanned and smooth, his skin rippled with row after row of well toned muscles. His abdomen was flat with a few stray curls of dark hair that disappeared beneath the unbuttoned waistband of his jeans. His bare feet were braced wide apart in a fighting stance. One hand rested on the door while the other was fisted at his side. High up on his shoulder, she saw the Marine Corps tattoo that she vividly remembered tracing with her tongue one memorable night.

Mercy. She actually *felt* heat streaming through her body. Every nerve ending went to full attention, and she knew that if he so much as touched her, she'd splinter into a thousand pieces.

Oh, she hoped he would.

His pale blue eyes watched her, and Kelly licked dry lips before speaking, desperately praying her voice would work.

"Maybe I should have called," she said finally.

"No," he said, and his voice scraped along her spine, sending goose bumps racing up and down her arms. "It's fine. I was about to go for a run—"

"Oh, then I'll—" Leave? She didn't want to leave.

"No," he said quickly. "It's okay. I'm just surprised to see you, that's all."

Of course he was surprised, she told herself. He'd left her only an hour ago with the promise that they'd meet tomorrow to talk some more. But she hadn't been able to sit still once he was gone. She'd waited eighteen months to see him again, and now that he was home, she didn't want to wait another minute.

"I know we said tomorrow," she said with a shrug, "but I thought…why put off till tomorrow what we could—?" She stopped, smiled and shrugged again. "You know."

"Yeah." He shoved his free hand into his pocket, and Kelly's gaze was drawn to the action. Naturally, she also noted the distinct bulge in his jeans, and another shiver coursed through her. Her knees were shaky, so she locked them in place to keep from melting into a tidy puddle in front of him.

"Where's the baby?" he asked.

"Uh, Kieran's staying with her." Thankfully, she had *one* brother at least who was a romantic at heart. He'd come as soon as she'd called and hadn't said a word when she told him where she was going. He'd only said that she should take her time, and that he was prepared to spend the night if she needed him to.

Of course, if Jeff didn't make her feel a bit more welcome pretty soon, she could be home again in ten minutes.

As if he knew just what she was thinking, he stood back, held the door wider and said, "Come in."

That's a start, she thought and stepped past him into the shadowy interior of the hotel room. The curtains were open on the sliding glass doors leading to the balcony, and moonlight poured into the room. The sheer white drapes ruffled in the ocean breeze and almost looked like ghosts writhing in the darkness.

The door closed behind her, and she felt Jeff step up close, pause, then move past her, farther into the room. He flipped a switch on the wall, and a small pool of lamplight banished the shadows.

Kelly swung her shoulder purse off her arm and tossed it onto the closest chair. Now that she was here, she wasn't at all sure where to start. She ran her damp hands down the legs of her jeans and told herself to say something. Heck, say *anything*.

"I know Emily was a big shock..." Well, *duh*.

"Yeah," he said, taking a step toward her, then stopping again. "You could say that."

"Jeff, I would have told you earlier if I'd had any way of getting in touch with you."

"I know that."

"And I'm sorry my brothers were there."

"Can't blame 'em," he said stiffly. "I figure my name hasn't exactly been popular around here for the last year and a half."

That was putting it mildly, she thought. Ever since she'd found out she was pregnant, her brothers had wanted nothing less than either a marriage—or Jeff's head on a plate. And they really hadn't cared which it came down to, either.

But that decision wasn't up to them, as she'd spent the past eighteen months telling them. This was between she and Jeff. No one else got a vote here.

"Let's leave them out of this for now, okay?" she asked, not really wanting to talk about her brothers at the moment.

He nodded and pinned her with a look that nearly set fire to her jeans. "Trust me. I'm not thinking about your brothers right now."

Oh, man. Kelly swallowed hard and walked toward him, one slow step at a time. "What are you thinking about?" she asked, and was amazed that she'd managed to squeeze that many words past the knot of pure, soul-deep hunger lodged in her throat.

He shook his head. "You know damn well what I'm thinking about, Kel. The same thing I've been thinking about and dreaming about for the last eighteen months."

"You, too?" she asked before she could stop herself. It probably wasn't playing the game to admit to a man just how badly you wanted him. But then again, who was playing here?

She took another step and came within reaching distance. His gaze moved over her face, her hair, her body like the tenderest of lover's touches, and her heartbeat quickened into double time.

"Every night," he said, his voice a low scrape of sound in the stillness, "whenever I closed my eyes, you were there. Your scent. Your taste."

Her knees wobbled dangerously.

"Your touch," he whispered, and lifted one hand to smooth his fingertips along the line of her cheek and jaw.

She trembled and fought for breath.

"It's been a long time," she said softly, her gaze locking with his.

"Too damn long," he agreed, and cupped the back of her neck with one hand, drawing her closer still.

She went willingly, laying her palms against his chest, feeling the hard, solid warmth of him. His heartbeat pounded quickly beneath one hand, and she knew her own heart was keeping time. Her blood felt hot and thick in her veins. Her head spun dizzily at his touch, and her breasts ached.

Kelly stared up into those blue eyes of his and read the hunger written there. Seeing his desire, so naked, so pure, touched a match to her insides and ignited an inferno within. Slowly, so slowly, the expectation was darn near painful, he lowered his head toward hers and she rose up to meet him.

This, she thought. This was why she'd come. This was why she hadn't been able to wait until tomorrow. She'd needed to have his hands on her. Needed to kiss and be kissed. Needed to hold and be held. Needed to lie beneath him, feeling him fill the emptiness inside.

And then his mouth came down on hers, and she stopped thinking. Her brain clicked off and her body clicked on. Sensation rippled through her, and she slid her palms up his chest and around his neck. Holding on to him tightly, she felt his arms slide around her and lock like twin steel bands, pinning her to his body with an easy strength she remembered all too clearly.

He parted her lips with his tongue and claimed

her anew. Breath mingling, sighs exchanged, their tongues met in a clashing dance of need and want. He shifted one hand to the back of her head, threading his fingers through her hair and holding her for his kiss. A kiss that gave, as well as took. She clung to him, tasting him, teasing him, aligning her body along his. And it wasn't nearly enough. There were too many clothes separating them. She needed to feel his skin against hers.

His hands swept around and up, cupping her breasts, thumbing her nipples through the soft angora sweater she wore. Kelly tore her mouth free of his and moaned gently at his touch. "Jeff..."

"I know, baby," he muttered thickly. "Me, too. I need to feel you. All of you. Now."

"Yes," she murmured, opening her eyes briefly to look up at him. "Now. Please."

Jeff's hands dropped to the hem of her sweater, and in one swift move, he had it up and over her head. Tossing it to one side, he ran his hands up and down her back while his gaze locked on her lace-covered breasts. Fuller, he thought. Rounder than before. And still so damn perfect.

She trembled against him, and that gentle movement echoed inside him. Reverently, he lifted both hands to the front clasp between her breasts and deftly undid it. She sucked in a huge gulp of air as the bra came loose and stood perfectly still when he scooped it off her shoulders and down her arms.

"Beautiful," he whispered, and cupped her breasts in his palms.

"Jeff..." she said on a sigh.

His thumbs and forefingers tweaked her already rigid nipples, tugging and pulling gently until her breath came short and fast. She reached out and held on to his forearms, curling her fingers into his skin until her trim nails dug into his flesh. Then he dipped his head and gave into the urge riding him. Taking first one nipple and then the other into his mouth, he tasted her, rolling the sensitive tips with his tongue, swirling across her skin, luxuriating in the feel of her beneath his mouth.

"Oh, my," she whispered. "I missed you so much." And she held on tighter even while she arched into him, offering herself to him, silently demanding he take more, give more.

So he did. He suckled her, drawing on those pink tips until she quivered in his grasp and only his hands at her waist were holding her upright. And when she groaned, deep and low, he straightened up and looked down into her eyes. Keeping their gazes locked, he unbuttoned her jeans and pulled the zipper down. She smiled at him. A soft, small, knowing smile and then returned the favor.

She slowly undid the buttons on his fly, and each time her knuckles brushed his skin, he sucked in another gulp of air and knew it would never be enough.

She freed him from his jeans and curled her fingers around his hard flesh. Jeff clenched his jaw and pulled air in through gritted teeth as he slid one hand down the front of her jeans and beneath her silk panties to cup her heat.

The smile on her face died instantly, but her fingers continued to work their magic on his flesh as he delved first one finger and then two into her hot center.

She rocked her hips against his hand, lifting up, moving so that he could touch her more fully, more completely.

"Jeff," she whispered, "I can't...I can't breathe."

"Then don't," he told her, his own voice tight. "Just feel." He smoothed the tip of a finger across her most sensitive spot, and she groaned, adjusting her stance to give him more access. Again and again, he touched her, rousing her, pushing her higher and higher, all the while trying to control his own response to her hands on him.

Her breath came fast and furious. Her body trembled. And when she cried out his name and fell against him, shaking with the force of the climax pounding through her, he carefully eased her down onto the floor. There he whisked off her clothes, got rid of his own and paused to grab a condom from the pocket of his jeans. When he was protected, he pushed himself inside her warmth and relished the feel of her legs lifting and coming around his waist.

This, he thought, feeling her body surround him, hold him, this was what he'd waited for. What he'd missed. This one woman. This one place where everything else in the world fell away.

He'd lived through misery and combat and loneliness, but here with her, none of it mattered. She held on to him, her hands running up and down his back as she urged, "Again, Jeff. Take me there again. It's been so long."

"Again," he repeated, lifting his head to look down into her eyes as his own climax hovered just out of reach. "And again. I'll never stop," he promised, meaning every word.

He'd thought about this for too long. Waited for it. Dreamed about it. And now that she was here, in his arms, her breath dusting against his face, he had to have her. He worked her body with his fingers, his hands. Touching, soothing, stroking, plunging. No rest. No stopping. He couldn't get enough of her and felt in her response that she felt the same.

Plunging in and out of her warmth, he stoked the fires within them both until they were engulfed in the flames. Thought fled, only hunger remained and still they touched and kissed and stroked.

His body tightened, his control slipped and she held him close, lifting her hips, racing to meet the climax crashing down on her. And when he thought he would lose his mind with the want, she said on a sigh, "Oh now, Jeff. Hold me."

He held her tightly, took her mouth with his and as her body quickened around his, he surrendered and rode the wave of his own completion, nestled safely in her arms.

Six

"Wow," Kelly murmured when she found her voice again.

"That about says it," Jeff agreed, and slowly, like a man afraid to move too quickly, rolled to one side of her. Keeping her close, he wrapped one arm around her and held her tightly to him.

She ran the flat of her hand across his chest and paused to feel the rapid beat of his heart. Smiling to herself, she cuddled in, nestling her head on his shoulder. Okay, maybe that hadn't solved anything. Maybe they still had problems to resolve and questions to answer. But by heaven, it had been wonderful. Just to be with him again.

"Glad you dropped by," Jeff said, and his voice rumbled through his chest like the echo of a passing train.

"Yeah," she said, tipping her head back to look up at him. "Me, too. By the way, nice floor."

One corner of his mouth lifted into a quirk of a smile. "Nothing but the best from me."

It figured that with a perfectly good bedroom just steps away, she and Jeff would end up on the plushly carpeted floor. It had always been like that between them. From the moment they'd met.

Well, she corrected silently, from the moment she'd regained consciousness to discover this gorgeous Marine giving her mouth-to-mouth resuscitation. She hardly recalled getting hit in the head by a stray surfboard. She certainly didn't remember sinking beneath the waves and swallowing half the ocean. But everything else about that day was etched in living, brilliant color in her memory.

Stretched out on the sand, someone's mouth on hers. She coughed, opened her eyes and looked up into a pair of blue eyes so pale, so clear it was as if she could see right through them into the hunk's soul. Then, as coughing spasms wracked her, he held on to her, soothing, stroking, gently whispering words of encouragement that reached into her heart and eased away the fear.

He'd saved her life, everyone said. She heard the smattering of applause from their bathing-suit-clad audience. But all she focused on was him. There was something between them, even then. And when he took her to lunch and then dinner, that something grew, blossoming out of nothingness to envelop them both in a wild, rare burst of passion and need that Kelly had never known before.

And for two weeks, they'd reveled in it and each other. It was as if they'd known each other before. Some other time, some other place. Not that she believed in that sort of past-life thing. But what other explanation was there for the connection that only strengthened with each passing day?

The sex had been incredible, but safe. They'd both been careful. And yet…as the saying went, "Life found a way." He hadn't been gone more than two weeks when Kelly discovered she was pregnant. In a weird sort of way, she hadn't even been surprised. It was as if what they'd experienced, what they'd found together was just too big to be contained.

"Kelly," he said, bringing her wandering

thoughts back to the present, "we still have to talk."

"I know," she said, skimming her hand down across his chest and back up again.

He sucked in a gulp of air and captured her hand, holding it tightly. "Keep doing that and we won't get much talking done."

Truth be told, she'd just as soon put off the talking. There was bound to be another argument. Because no matter what he said, she didn't want to get married. Marriage had never been in her plans. Of course, growing up with four bossy older brothers probably had a lot to do with that. Still, it was probably best to get this settled between them.

"Okay," she said, surrendering to the inevitable. Pushing up into a sitting position, she looked down at him and said, "Let's talk."

His gaze swept over her body, lingering on her breasts for a moment, before he sighed and raised up on both elbows. "You don't make it easy on a man, do you?"

"Dressed or undressed, there's nothing about this that's going to be easy, Jeff."

"It could be."

"If I do what you want." Typical, she thought. Hadn't she been dealing with four males all of her life? She'd learned early that if you wanted to have smooth sailing, all you had to do was agree with them. But smooth sailing wasn't all it was cracked up to be. She'd just as soon have waves as surrender her own opinions.

And heaven knows, she was plenty used to going up against a hardheaded male.

"It's not just what I want," Jeff said, meeting her gaze squarely. "It's what's best for Emily."

"Really?" A brief, red-hot spurt of anger shot through her, chasing away any lingering warm fuzzies she might have been feeling. She pushed her hair back from her face and glared at him. "You've known your daughter for about five hours and you already know what's best for her?"

"I didn't say that, exactly."

"Yes, you did."

"No, I didn't."

"And how do you come by this spectacular piece of insight?" she went on, warming to the attack. "By benefit of your far superior male brain?"

"Come on, Kelly," he said, eyes narrowing.

"No, really," she said, and stood up, preferring to be on her feet for the argument that was headed her way at a fast clip. "That's what you meant."

"Damn it, I did not."

"Don't curse at me," she warned him. "And yeah, you did."

"So now you know what I mean even when I don't?"

She wagged one finger at him and shook her head, sending those curls of hers into a wild dance around her face. "You don't think I know what you mean, but I do and I think you know I know."

"Huh?" Jeff's features twisted as he tried to follow that little piece of logic. But Kelly wasn't listening. She was already on a tear. Damn, this evening had gone to hell in a hurry.

First the gift of her appearing at his door when he most needed her. Then a mind-numbing reunion. Now this. For pete's sake, what did he do that was so damn terrible? Was a proposal from him so repellent?

"Don't you play all innocent with me, Jeff Hunter," she was saying as she marched—buck naked—back and forth in front of him.

Boy, it didn't do much for a man's concentration. How in the hell was he supposed to focus on an argument when he was watching those breasts of hers? Not to mention that finely curved behind?

Then she started talking again and spoiled the moment completely.

"You want us to get married because you have

some old-world notion that it's the honorable thing to do.''

''Well, it is,'' he countered, silently objecting to the term *old world.* Hell, was it that out of date to be a decent guy? To stand up and take responsibility for your actions?

Standing up, he faced her on his own two feet. Folding his arms across his chest, he kept his gaze fixed on her while she continued to pace.

''Fine,'' she said. ''You did the honorable thing. You offered. But I don't *want* to get married.''

''Why the hell not?''

That stopped her cold.

She planted both hands at her bare hips and tapped the toes of one foot soundlessly against the carpet. ''Are you serious? For one thing, we hardly know each other!''

Eyebrows arched, he glanced at the floor, then back to her. ''I think we know each other pretty damn well.''

''That's sex, Jeff.''

''Yeah, I know what it is.'' And if he was any judge, they were damn good at it.

''Good sex really isn't considered a basis for a long-standing relationship.''

''God, I hate that word,'' he muttered.

''What word?''

"Relationship," he snapped. "Everyone tosses that word around these days to cover everything from a parent and a child to married couples. Relationship problems. How to build a successful relationship." He shook his head. "What we're talking about here is getting married and providing *our daughter* with two parents."

"She *has* two parents."

"I mean two parents together."

"Oh, really?" she asked, tipping her head to one side and staring at him thoughtfully. "Together? So you're saying if we got married, you'd leave the Corps. Leave Force Recon and be a regular nine-to-five husband and father?"

A cold chill crawled up his spine at the thought of spending the rest of his life tucked away behind a desk. He'd go out of his mind in nothing flat. He loved his job. Hell, he was good at it. And he wasn't at all sure he could give it up. Not even for Kelly.

And what did that make him?

"Uh-huh," she said, obviously reading his thoughts by the expression on his face. "I thought not. So what is this 'together' stuff?"

He scrubbed one hand across his face. "By together, I mean married. A couple. A family. With one name. A mom and a dad and a kid."

She sighed and shoved both hands through her hair, sculpting it back from her face, giving him a clear look at her high cheekbones, wide green eyes and lush mouth. Something inside him tightened. God, she was gorgeous. And Jeff wanted her again with a fierceness that shook him to his bones.

Her hands dropped to her sides, and she looked at him as if willing him to understand. Which he didn't.

"Jeff," she said in a weary voice, "I don't want a husband. *Any* husband."

Well, he thought, at least it wasn't just *him* she was refusing. It wasn't personal. This was something that went deeper for her. He didn't know if that was a good thing or not, either. On the one hand, if it wasn't *him* she had a problem with, he still had a chance to convince her. But if she simply had a problem with marriage, it was going to be hard to get past that.

And it wasn't as if this was easy for *him,* either. Hell, if there was one thing in life he'd never been interested in, it was marriage. He just wasn't the kind of man women looked at and thought, Ah, husband material.

He was more the type for one-night stands and the occasional spectacular weekend. Until Kelly, that is. Ever since those two weeks with her, Jeff had been haunted by thoughts of what-if. It wasn't just the fact of Emily's presence that had him wondering about a life with Kelly. It was her and how she made him feel when he was with her.

Emily had simply speeded up the process.

Marriage itself was still a terrifying prospect. But he'd never be able to look in a mirror again if he didn't do everything possible to get her to agree. A man wasn't worth much if he didn't stand up and take responsibility for his actions.

"Hell, Kelly," he said, folding his arms across his chest and giving her a half smile, "I'm not just *any* husband."

One corner of her mouth quirked as she shook her head. "Good one."

"Thanks," he said, "I try."

As she blew out a breath, those curls danced above her forehead and Jeff smiled at the picture she made. Not many women could stand there stone naked and argue without the slightest hint of embarrassment. Yep. Kelly was one in a million.

"I don't want to fight anymore, Jeff. That's not why I came here tonight."

"Why did you come?" he asked softly.

She sighed, waved her hands to indicate her nudity and admitted, "To see you."

"I'm glad."

"Are you?" she asked. "Even with the arguing?"

"Baby, I've missed that about you, too," he admitted, walking across the room to stop directly in
front of her. Reaching out, he rubbed his palms up
and down her upper arms and smiled to himself
when she sort of leaned in toward him. "There's
nobody I'd rather argue with."

"Hmm…"

"Don't believe me?" he asked, smiling. "Trust
me, Travis, Deke and J.T. don't look nearly as
good as you do when their tempers are up."

"You're a real sweet talker, aren't you?" she
asked, that quirk tugging at her mouth again.

"When I have to be."

Her smile faded at that.

"Jeff…" She lifted her gaze to his, and he
found himself falling into the depths of her green
eyes. At that moment, he would have promised her
anything.

"Yeah?"

"Could we stop arguing—just for tonight?"

An easy enough thing to promise. Hell, he didn't
want to argue anymore, either. Not after waiting a
year and a half just to get his hands on her again.
Besides, there would be plenty enough time to go
over his proposal in the next two weeks. He wasn't

a man to give up easy and he figured she knew that.

"Sure," he said, and pulled her close, holding her up against him, reveling in the soft feel of her body aligned along his. When her arms went around his waist, he breathed deep, drawing her scent inside him where he would keep it, along with the memory of this moment, forever. "I think we can do that."

She nestled in close, laying her head on his chest, and Jeff rested his chin atop her head. They stood locked together in the moonlit shadows and measured the passing seconds in heartbeats.

Hours later, Kelly woke up alone in the king-size bed. One arm stretched out, reaching for Jeff, but all she found was what felt like an acre of cool sheets. She blinked and sat up, trying to wake, wondering where he'd gone.

Grabbing up the closest piece of clothing, she slipped one of Jeff's T-shirts over her head and smiled to herself when the hem came down to the middle of her thighs. A big man, she told herself and smiled again, remembering just how well she'd relearned that body of his during the past few hours.

Her muscles ached, but if a minor discomfort

was the price to be paid for feeling as well loved as she did, then it was worth it. No wonder the military wives she'd come to know in the past year or two never seemed to mind their husbands being deployed. Oh, boy, when they came back home, they more than made up for their absence!

Sex with Jeff had always been intense, explosive. But tonight… She inhaled sharply and blew it out again, trying to steady herself. Tonight, he'd outdone himself. Tonight, they'd crossed the line from ''pretty amazing'' into ''downright awesome.''

His scent still clung to her, and Kelly had the feeling that it might never wear off. It was as though he'd been trying to burn himself into her mind and body and soul.

And darn if he hadn't, she thought, stepping out of the bedroom into the darkened living room. Her knees went weak just recalling the mind-numbing climaxes she'd experienced in his arms. And the memories alone were enough to thicken her blood and get it coursing hot and heavy through her veins.

''For pity's sake,'' she muttered, astonished at her own eagerness. Until Jeff had come into her life, she hadn't been very impressed with sex. Frankly, she'd always much preferred sleeping.

Her one or two encounters in college really had not prepared her for the reality that was Jeff Hunter.

She'd had no idea she could have such an...*appetite*. Her craving for him seemed endless, bottomless. It was as though the more he touched her, the more she needed. And that realization shook her, hard.

Because Jeff wasn't satisfied being her lover. He'd made up his mind to be her husband.

Seven

A warning bell went off in the back of her mind, and Kelly knew that sooner or later she and Jeff were going to have to settle this marriage business once and for all. But now, she told herself, wasn't the time. Now she only wanted to find him. Hold him. Feel his arms go around her and pretend that this was all just a repeat of their first two weeks together.

Her gaze swept the dark room and noted instantly the billowing curtains fluttering at the open sliding glass doors. Moonlight was dim now, as morning looked to be just an hour or so away. She moved closer to the tiny balcony and noticed the stars fading in a slowly lightening sky. Then her gaze locked on Jeff's broad, bare back.

Worn, faded blue jeans were his one concession to clothing and they clung to his rear and long legs so closely that he looked even sexier than he would have naked. He stood, one hip cocked, hands on the rail, staring out at the smooth-as-glass ocean. The scent of the sea wafted through the doors at her, and she lifted her chin into the soft breeze, feeling damp, cool fingers draw her hair back from her face.

Taking a deep, fortifying breath, she stepped out onto the balcony and took up a spot beside him.

He wasn't startled by her presence, and Kelly had the eerie feeling that he'd known all along that she'd been there behind him. Must be some sort of sixth sense a man acquired after spending years fighting for his life. That thought flitted through her mind, and she quailed from it. She didn't want to think about Jeff in danger. Jeff, hiding in jungles, dodging bullets from an unseen enemy. She'd managed to avoid imagining such scenarios during the year and a half they were apart and she sure as heck didn't want to think about them now.

"You're up early," she said, keeping her gaze fixed on the horizon and the sweep of pale pink color just beginning to reach across the sky from the east.

"Used to it, I guess," he said, keeping his voice as soft as the morning. He glanced at her briefly, then looked back at the ever changing ocean. "My T-shirt looks good on you."

"Thanks. I, uh, couldn't find my clothes," she said on a chuckle.

He smiled and Kelly's gaze locked on his profile. High cheekbones, a strong jaw and a nose that looked as if it had been broken more than once, all combined to make a face so ruggedly chiseled, Jeff was a poster boy for God's best work. He turned to look at her, and the look in his eyes sent a pang of emotion shooting straight into her heart.

"What?" she asked, reaching over to cover one of his hands with hers. "What is it?"

"I've been thinking," he admitted. "It's a good time for it. Quiet. Just before the day's born."

"And?" she asked hesitantly, hoping to heaven he wasn't going to start on the whole marriage thing again so soon.

"And," he repeated on a sigh, "I was wondering. What did you look like pregnant?"

The question was so not what she was expecting, Kelly only stared at him for a long minute. Then when it fully registered, she gave a short, rueful laugh and shook her head. "Like a beach ball," she said. "Short and round."

In fact, through most of her pregnancy, she'd been seriously grateful that Jeff couldn't see her. Short women and pregnancy were not a good match, she thought and remembered how she used to stare at the taller moms-to-be at her doctor's office with such envy. Even at their biggest, those women had somehow managed to look...aglow. While Kelly, on the other hand, had looked like a barrel with legs.

She'd often wondered if Jeff would have been appalled or entranced by the changes in her body, but the coward in her was simply pleased she'd never have to find out.

"I bet you looked beautiful."

She laughed then, a loud, short burst of sound that had her clapping one hand over her mouth. After all, it was a little early to be waking everyone else at the hotel.

"Not even close," she said. "My brothers insisted that if there was just some way to rig the lights, they'd hire me out as a blimp."

He scowled at that, and Kelly was instantly sorry she'd mentioned her brothers. "They were just teasing me," she said quickly.

"Yeah, right," he muttered, more to himself

than to her, and added, "at least they were here for you," so softly she almost missed it.

"Jeff…"

"Did you hate me?" he asked bluntly, and this time kept his gaze fixed on the water below them. "For leaving you pregnant and alone?"

"No," she said, pulling him around until he was forced to look at her. She had to convince him of this, if nothing else. "Of course not. First," she reminded him, "I wasn't alone. My family was here."

"Yeah, and they were thrilled with me."

"This isn't about them."

"You're right," he said. "This is about you and me, and I need to know. Did you hate me?"

She looked directly into his eyes, willing him to read the truth in hers. Then she said very slowly, "No. I never hated you for making me pregnant."

Some of the tension seeped out of his body, and she went on quickly, hoping to ease away the rest. "It's not as if I had nothing to do with it, you know."

A small, too brief smile quirked his mouth and was gone again. "Yeah, I remember."

"It wasn't either of our faults that the condom failed."

"I'm still thinking about suing the company," he growled.

"Pointless," she told him. "It says right on the box that they're ninety-eight percent effective. They gave themselves an out clause."

"Hmm...clever *and* ineffective."

Stewing about how and why a condom failed was useless. She'd learned that herself eighteen months ago. Better to just deal with the reality and accept it. "Jeff, what happened, happened for a reason."

"You believe that?"

"I do," she said, and put every ounce of her conviction into the words. She meant it. Every time she looked into Emily's little face, that feeling grew. There was a reason for that baby. A reason she'd been conceived against all odds. A reason she'd come into the world at all.

Just because Kelly didn't know what that reason was, didn't negate it.

"Wish I knew what it was," he murmured.

"Does it really matter?" she asked, and hoped he'd say no. For Emily's sake, she didn't want her baby's father to be regretting the child's existence.

A long minute passed before he answered her, and Kelly didn't realize she was holding her breath until it whooshed out of her chest when he spoke.

"No, it doesn't."

"Good," she said, feeling relief sweep through her. For Emily's sake, she told herself. It was only Emily's feelings she was concerned with here.

Turning her around in his grasp, Jeff faced the ocean again and drew her close, her back to his front. Wrapping his arms around her, he held her tightly and said, "Tell me about it."

"It?" she asked, reaching up to lay her hands on his crossed forearms.

"Your pregnancy. Labor. Delivery." He shrugged and she felt the motion ripple through her. "I want to know everything. Everything I missed."

His voice carried a silent plea that arrowed into her heart in a swift, sure thrust. He *had* missed so much, she thought. He'd come home from a series of dangerous missions to discover a daughter he'd known nothing about. And now he was trying, the only way he could, to become a part of that little girl's life. To know her as her mother did. To be more than the man who'd created her.

To be her father.

Kelly's heart ached sweetly, and she caressed his arms with gentle, soothing strokes.

Somewhere off to the east, the sun was rising, reaching out with warm hands to caress the night sky and draw pale, soft colors onto its surface. Five stories below them, a handful of surfers in wet suits were already in the cold water, paddling out on the glassy ocean, waiting, hoping for waves to begin a slow curl toward shore.

And while the world woke up, Kelly talked.

Jeff listened and as she spoke, his mind created images to go along with the words. In his imagination, he saw Kelly, round with his child. Going to work, playing with the kindergartners she so clearly adored. Unwrapping clumsily wrapped presents for the baby. Hearing the baby names twenty five-year-olds had come up with.

He saw her in the doctor's office. Felt her excitement at her first ultrasound when she actually *saw* Emily inside her. And he also felt a flash of regret that he hadn't been there, holding her hand, staring at that screen and trying to make out the features of his child on a fuzzed-out screen. He listened to her talk about her brothers and tried not to resent the fact that it had been the Rogan brothers who'd been there to help her, not him. They'd mowed her grass, taken her grocery shopping, set up Emily's crib and painted the nursery. They'd been there for their little sister at the most important time of her life, while Jeff hadn't even had a clue as to what was going on.

A flash of useless, directionless anger shot through him with the force of mortar fire, lighting up his insides. Even knowing that it wasn't his fault…that he hadn't known…didn't seem to help.

When she described her labor, though, Jeff was torn between being grateful he'd missed the opportunity to see her in pain and more regret that his hadn't been the hand she'd clung to. No, that job had fallen to Kevin Rogan. The oldest brother. The man who'd taken his first opportunity to punch Jeff dead in the face.

And damn if Jeff could find it in him to blame the guy.

"Then," Kelly was saying, and he gave his attention back to her, "Emily was there and the doctor was holding her up like a bowling trophy." She laughed and Jeff smiled to hear it. "And Emily, she opened her eyes and I swear, Jeff, she looked right at me. The doctor swore that she couldn't see anything, but I know different. Emily looked at me as if asking, 'What the heck is going on around here, Mom? What's all the noise about?'"

He chuckled and rested his chin atop her head, seeing it all through her eyes, wishing he'd been there to see it all for himself.

"Then he laid her across my chest," she said, her voice so soft he had to strain to hear it. "And she stared into my eyes, took hold of my finger in the tightest grip you could imagine and in that instant, she slipped right into my soul."

Tears stung his eyes and Jeff was so surprised, he blinked frantically to keep them at bay.

A long minute passed before she sighed and told him fondly, "Kevin was crying like a baby."

Jeff scowled at the thought of the man who clearly hated the sight of him, being the one to witness the miracle of Emily's birth.

"He pretended he wasn't, of course," she was saying. "No Marine, on pain of death, would ever admit to that, but then you know that, don't you?"

"Damn right," he agreed, and blinked more quickly.

"I wish you could have been there," she murmured.

A cold, tight fist squeezed his heart until it felt as though it were being wrung from his chest. "So do I, baby," he said softly, and kissed the top of her head. In fact, he knew that for the rest of his days, he would be sorry he'd missed out on so much. It was a time that could never be recaptured. The magic couldn't be revisited.

No. There was nothing he could do about the past.

But the present and the future were up for grabs.

His mind raced, going first in one direction, then another, trying to find places, spots where he could infiltrate Kelly's and his daughter's lives. He wanted—no, *needed*—to be involved in what was happening now.

God knew, he didn't know anything about family life. And even less about children. But that little girl was his *baby*. A part of him. And he wouldn't be denied the chance to be in her life. To have her know him. To be something more than he ever had been before.

And then it hit him.

Keeping his voice even, he asked, "Who watches Emily when you're at work?"

She stiffened slightly in his arms, and Jeff knew she was all set to get defensive. Well, he'd just have to disarm her. Shouldn't be any more hazardous than dealing with a land mine.

"Don't you start, too," she warned, her voice as stiff as her posture.

"Start what?"

"Kevin is forever giving me grief about Emily being in day care for half a day. I don't need the two of you double-teaming me."

"Hey, hey. Don't shoot!"

"What?"

"Take your finger off the trigger, baby," he said quietly, turning her in his arms again until he could look down into her eyes. No way was he going to be set alongside Kevin Rogan in her eyes as though they were a team or something. "I'm not in a position to give you grief over any decision you've made for Emily."

She relaxed just a bit, but not by much. "Okay," she said, and ducked her head briefly before looking up at him again. "But you *do* have more right to an opinion than Kevin."

Damn straight, he wanted to say, but wisely, didn't.

"I was just asking," he said.

She nodded. "You know I teach at St. Matthew's."

"Yeah…" He remembered her telling him all about her class at the local Catholic school.

"Well," she continued, "the teachers there also run a day care for the parents of students, and Emily spends her mornings there while I'm at class." Then, as if he was going to attack, she hurried on. "It's a wonderful setup. I can visit her at recess and naptime. The nun in charge is a lovely woman and she really loves the kids. Gives them plenty of attention.''

While she described the school and day-care center, Jeff's mind wandered. Hell, he'd been raised mostly in a Catholic orphanage in St. Louis, so he figured he had more firsthand knowledge of how well nuns looked after children than she did. But then, Kelly wasn't aware of most of his childhood circumstances and now wasn't the time to give her more details.

"I'm convinced," he said, only to slow down the rush of words. "Besides, I only wanted to know because—'' Did he really want to do this? Yes, he thought. He did. "I was thinking. Maybe while I'm home on leave, I could take care of Emily while you're at work. Give me a chance to get to know her and for her to know me."

Kelly looked at him for a long, thoughtful minute, and he would have given plenty to know what exactly she was thinking. Then she spoke and the mystery was solved.

"You want to take care of her? Alone? By yourself?"

"Yeah," he said, unconsciously straightening up under her steady regard. What?

"But, Jeff, you've told me yourself that you've never had much to do with kids."

"I was one once—doesn't that count?"

She smiled. "Do you even know anything about babies?"

"I know they can't breathe underwater," he said, keeping a straight face.

"Very funny."

"I know they need to eat. They need to be changed. And they sleep a lot."

"Uh-huh."

She didn't look convinced.

"Look, Kel," he said, "how hard can it be? I'm a Marine, for God's sake. The U.S. government trusts me with million-dollar machinery. Surely I can be trusted to spoon mashed-up bananas into my daughter's mouth."

"I don't know," she said. "I mean, of course I want you to spend time with Emily. I want her to know you. I want you to be able to see just how special she is." Kelly laid both open palms on his chest, and he wondered if she could feel the thundering beat of his heart.

"It's just—"

"You're worried."

"A little."

"I can do this, Kelly," he said, needing to prove to both her and himself that he was right. "Trust me."

"I do trust you—"

"Then it's settled?"

She chewed nervously at her bottom lip, and his gaze followed the motion. His body stirred into life as he planned on biting that lip himself. Once he had her answer.

"I guess so," she said, forcing a smile she clearly didn't feel.

"Excellent," Jeff said. It didn't matter that "I guess so" wasn't exactly a glowing approval. He'd take what he could get. Gripping her tightly about the waist, he lifted her off her feet long enough to plant a long, satisfying kiss on the mouth that drove him to distraction. When he set her back down, she blinked up at him.

"Tomorrow morning, you'll come over to my place, then?"

That was one way of handling the situation, he thought, but he had another way in mind. They had a long, lazy Sunday ahead of them. And if he worked this just right, he'd spend the night lying in Kelly's bed at her house. Then he'd be there, ready to step in and care for their daughter first thing in the morning.

Still, probably a good idea if he didn't throw his plan at her all at once.

"You bet, baby," he said, pulling her close

enough that she couldn't help but feel the rock-solid proof of how much he needed her again.

Her eyes widened, then went smoky dark, and he knew she was feeling everything he was. Good. He wanted to make himself indispensable to her over the next thirty days. He wanted to prove to her that he could be everything she and his daughter needed.

"But for now," he pointed out, bending his head and stopping just a breath away from kissing her, "we've got a long Sunday with lots of hours to kill." He leaned closer, his lips tasting, tugging at hers. "Got any ideas?"

"Oh," she whispered, lifting her arms to encircle his neck. "A few."

Eight

"Emily's crying," Kelly said, and gave Jeff a nudge.

"Hmm? What?" He came awake instantly and sat up. His gaze swept Kelly's bedroom, and it only took a moment to remember where he was and why he was there. Oh, yeah. His plan. Well, it had worked. He'd spent the night with her at her house so that he could be on hand when Emily woke up.

Which, apparently, was now.

A cry sounded out again from the next room, and he smiled to himself.

"Go," Kelly mumbled. "Bond."

Swinging his legs off the bed, he jumped up, grabbed up his jeans from the crumpled heap on the floor and tugged them on. He looked at Kelly, still lying, face into her pillow, auburn curls spread across the spring-green linen, looking like a fire in a meadow.

Jeff just enjoyed the view for a long minute, relishing the simple pleasure of waking up alongside her. Damn, but it felt good. Right. His plan had worked beautifully. He, Kelly and Emily had spent most of yesterday afternoon together, with he and his daughter becoming acquainted. Thankfully, she was a happy baby, with an outgoing personality that was more her mother than her father. She simply looked at Jeff as yet another conquest, completely expecting him to adore her as everyone else did.

Naturally, he did just that. A swell of pride filled him. Emily was the brightest child he'd ever seen. Well, all right, he thought, he hadn't been around enough children to make a real comparison. But anyone could see that she was clever and quick and so damn beautiful. She wore her heart in her eyes and every time she turned those big blue eyes on her daddy, he fell just a bit more in love with her. Her smile tugged at his heart, and her cries broke it.

Amazing really. He'd never known such all encompassing love before. Wouldn't have believed it possible if someone had told him about it. But he guessed folks were right. You just never knew what love really was until you had a child of your own.

From the next room, his delicate flower sent up a screech of disapproval loud enough to pry one of Kelly's eyes open. She looked up at him and without moving a muscle asked, "So are you going in to get her or what?"

"You bet, baby. I'm on my way." But before he did, he planted one knee on the mattress, leaned over and kissed the top of Kelly's head.

"I'd turn over and give you a real kiss," she murmured, her words muffled by the sheets, "but I don't want to move."

"Later," he said, knowing damn well that *he* was the reason she was so worn-out this morning. After all, it had been eighteen months since either one of them had had a marathon sex session. He grinned to himself at the memory of the long night before.

"'Kay," she said, and closed that eye again.

Climbing back off the bed, Jeff left the bedroom,

closing the door behind him before going into his daughter's nursery.

Everything a child could ever want littered the floor and was piled on the shelves lining the walls. Outside, dawn was just beginning to streak across the sky, and the pale, shadowy light was lost in the glow of the angel night light. Jeff flicked the small light off and looked into his daughter's furious expression.

"Well, then, morning, sweet pea," he crooned, and had the satisfaction of seeing that frown slide off her face to be replaced by a teary smile. And damn if he didn't feel better than he would have if some General had just pinned a medal to his chest.

Emily grabbed hold of the crib rails and worked her feet frantically, trying to scale the barrier between them. He saved her the trouble. Scooping her up into his arms, he grimaced a bit at the dampness clinging to her and said, "First things first, little girl. Let's get you a fresh set of drawers."

She laughed and talked to him while he changed her diaper and clumsily did up the snaps on a fresh pair of pajamas. The little built-in slippers about did him in. How was a man supposed to tuck squirmy little feet into the blasted things without having the toes of the jammies turned around toward her heels?

But when the mystery was finally solved and Emily was as fresh as she was going to get, he picked her up and carried her toward the kitchen. With the warm, solid weight of his daughter against his chest, Jeff determined that the rest of their day would pass uneventfully.

"Why isn't he answering the phone?" Kelly muttered, then pulled the receiver away from her ear to glare at it, as if this were all the phone's fault.

"Perhaps he's busy, dear," Sister Mary Angela offered.

"How long does it take to pick up the phone and say, 'Can't talk now'?" For heaven's sake, she'd called him an hour and a half ago and everything was fine. Where could he be? Why would he have taken Emily anywhere? And how was she going to stand being at school for another hour without finding out how things were going?

"Apparently, longer than he's got," the nun mused, smiling at the other woman's obvious case of nerves. "You *did* want Emily's father to be a part of her life, didn't you?"

"Yes, but—"

"And you *do* trust Jeff, don't you?"

Kelly blew out a breath. "Of course I do, Sister, it's just that—"

"It's just that you don't want to share your daughter?"

A guilty flush stole over her. Was that it? Was she being *jealous* of Emily's affections? No, Kelly thought. She refused to believe that. This was an honest-to-goodness, realistic worry. Her daughter was alone with her father for the first time, and he wasn't answering the stupid phone!

"Sister Angela," Kelly said, hanging up with another frosty look at the telephone, "Jeff's never been around babies before and—"

"He's an adult, Kelly. He'll figure it out."

"You know," Kelly said, a rueful grin curving her mouth, "you could let me get the whole complaint out of my mouth before shooting it down."

"No sense in wasting time, though, is there?" Sister Angela glanced at the wall clock in the school office. "Now, unless you want to try to bother your young man one more time, I'd suggest you rejoin your class. Recess is almost over."

"Bother, huh?" Kelly asked as she headed for the door.

The school principal's face took on the supremely patient expression she was famous for as she said, "He's only going to be alone with Emily for four hours today, my dear. What could possibly go wrong in four miserably short hours?"

"What else can go wrong?" Jeff muttered, wiping up the flood of orange juice racing across the kitchen table. He'd never seen a kid spill so much. "Spill proof cups, my ass," he muttered darkly as he tossed the small plastic cup into the sink. He hadn't seen this much liquid since the last time he'd been sent overseas on flood relief.

He glanced at his daughter and wondered fleetingly how Kelly kept up with the child. Hell, it must be something God gave women that He didn't give men. Just trying to ride herd on the little girl made him feel like he'd been on a ten-mile hike with a full pack. He was worn down to the ground. And he didn't have to worry about doing the laundry. He'd already had to change the baby's outfit three times in the past two hours.

But that wasn't the half of it. She'd shoved a half-chewed teething cracker into the VCR, ripped her mother's credit-card bill in half and chewed on the sports section of the newspaper.

And it wasn't even noon yet.

Plus, the phone kept ringing off the hook, as if he had time to worry about that. Maybe he wasn't cut out for this, he thought and found himself thinking fondly of slopping through a swamp with a half-dozen unfriendlies hot on his tail.

Then he glanced at Emily, and his doubts melted under the beam of that smile. She kicked her legs against the slats of her high chair, crowed delightedly and finished tossing banana slices across the room like tiny Frisbees. One of them hit him square in the forehead and while Emily giggled, Jeff sighed and wondered when it was exactly he'd lost control.

The first hour or so had been great. But things had pretty much gone downhill after that. Hell, maybe this hadn't been such a good idea. He'd never felt so damn useless in his life. Any other kind of situation, Jeff would be the man to jump in and take charge. But apparently, keeping a baby entertained was just a bit out of his reach.

"Recon, huh?" a deep voice from the back door asked.

Jeff swallowed the groan choking him and straightened up. Turning to face Kevin Rogan, he wondered just who in heaven or hell he'd ticked off lately. "Your point?" he asked.

Kevin stepped into the room, taking his Smokey Bear hat off and setting it on a relatively clean spot on the counter. "Thought you Recon guys were hot stuff.'' He paused and glanced around the room. Dark brown eyebrows lifted into high arches as he whistled and shook his head. ''Man, you should think about calling in air support. You're outgunned.''

Though he'd been thinking the same thing himself only a moment ago, hearing this guy say it aloud really stuck in his craw. ''I suppose you could do it better.''

''Hell,'' Kevin said, folding his arms across his chest, ''a blind monkey with both arms tied behind its back could do better.''

''Then you're overqualified, aren't you?'' Jeff asked as he walked across the room to his daughter and lifted her out of the chair. Emily laughed and clapped both banana-mushed hands to his cheeks. He ignored it and walked back toward the drill inspector who was so sure of himself. ''You talk a good game. Let's see what a D.I. can do, huh?''

''No problem,'' the other man said, and reached out for his niece. Too late, he noticed the bananas now decorating the front of his uniform blouse.

Jeff smiled. He felt better already.

Kelly parked the car in the driveway, noted her brother Kevin's car at the curb out front, then hur-

ried to the front door. Jeff and Kevin? Alone together? With only Emily to referee?

"Big mistake, Kelly," she muttered as she slid
the key into the lock and turned it. "You never
should have agreed to this. You were just asking
for troub—" Her voice trailed off as she opened
the door.

Stunned into silence, she stepped into what
looked like the aftereffects of a hurricane. Toys,
diapers, jars of baby food were scattered all across
the living room. And in the middle of the floor, his
head resting on the belly of a teddy bear, was
Kevin, in full uniform, sound asleep, still clutching
Emily's ring of plastic keys.

A soft snore caught her attention, and she shifted
her gaze to the couch. Jeff lay stretched out atop
the cushions, zonked out, with a sleeping Emily
tucked against his chest. His arms were wrapped
around her sturdy little body and she was sucking
her thumb, clearly content in her daddy's embrace.

Smiling to herself, Kelly leaned against the
arched doorjamb and just enjoyed the view. Her
daughter and the man she—what? Loved?

Her heart twisted in her chest, and a soft sigh
escaped her. Oh man. Lust she could handle. But
love? Love was something she hadn't really
counted on.

* * *

The next week slid past, with the three of them settling into a routine that was both comforting and a little scary for Kelly. One part of her loved the normalcy of it all. Of having Jeff there to help care for Emily. Of knowing that her daughter and Jeff were forming bonds that would last a lifetime. But on the other hand…

She was beginning to depend on Jeff and she didn't want to. Every once in a while, she caught a thoughtful gleam in his eye and Kelly knew he was still thinking about the proposal he'd made. They hadn't talked about it again and for that, she was grateful. But sooner or later, the subject would come up. He would want this settled between them before he left in three short weeks.

And Jeff wasn't the kind of man to take no as an answer without a battle.

"There's just no easy way out of this," she complained aloud as she folded yet another of Emily's freshly washed T-shirts.

From her walker, the baby gurgled something that Kelly was sure was meant as supportive. Then Emily went up on her toes, waved both arms and scooted forward half an inch on the carpeted floor.

"You'll be walking soon, won't you?" Kelly asked, and clutching the T-shirt in both hands, leaned back against the sofa cushions to watch her daughter. "Then it'll be school and your first date and then before I know it, you'll be getting married and leaving poor ol' Mom behind."

Emily leaned forward and gnawed on a bright pink plastic knob attached to the front of her walker.

"Yep," Kelly went on. "Your daddy will walk you down the aisle and when the ceremony's over, he'll go his way and I'll go mine." In her mind's eye, she saw it all. Emily, radiant in white, Jeff, still handsome and herself, alone.

"Now why do you suppose 'alone' suddenly feels so...*lonely?*" Kelly asked, and Emily continued to chew, uninterested in the conversation. "I never wanted to get married, you know. It's not that I don't want to marry your daddy. I just don't want another male in my life."

Emily blew a spit bubble.

"Your uncles have always been so darn bossy, and who needs that from one more guy?" Kelly scowled to herself, folded the now crumpled T-shirt and idly smoothed out the wrinkles. "Of course, Jeff really isn't the bossy type, is he?" she mused, remembering that he hadn't once given her grief over Emily's day care as her brothers did on a regular basis. And after that first day of caring for Emily, hadn't he gotten the hang of things? Hadn't he even cooked dinner for them twice in the past week?

This was a man used to doing for himself. He wasn't one to sit on a recliner and shout, "Bring me a beer." She smiled to herself at the thought. Jeff wasn't like any other man she'd ever known, and maybe that's what had her so worried. Because of him, she was even starting to rethink her "never marry" theory. And she wasn't at all sure she wanted that.

"First off," Travis drawled lazily as he reached for his bottle of beer, "you've got to figure out just what you want."

"That's easy," Jeff told him, "I want Kelly. And Emily. Haven't I just spent the last hour telling you that?"

Travis, Deke and J.T. sprawled on the couch, chairs and floor of the hotel suite. Jeff looked at them all, each in turn and smiled to himself. Four more unlikely friends you'd never meet. But they had become more than friends over the past few years. They'd become family.

Travis, one of six kids, hailed from a small town in Texas. Deke came from old-line Boston money. J.T. was the only child of a three-star General. And

Jeff, hell, the only family he'd ever had was here in this room.

The three of them looked at each other before looking back at Jeff. But Travis was the one who spoke up. "All right, then. What you've got to do is think of Kelly like you would any other target."

"Target?" he repeated.

"Hell, yes," Deke broke in. "Scope the situation out, plan your assault, then go in under cover of darkness."

"Sneak up on the enemy, er, Kelly," J.T. added, "until you've got her right where you want her."

Of course, he thought. Go with your strengths. And he'd had plenty of practice for this kind of thing. After all, trying to talk Kelly into marrying him would be every bit as dangerous as slipping undetected into enemy territory.

"You've got three weeks left, Jeff," Travis said in that slow-moving speech of his, "make 'em count, boy."

"Ooh-rah," Deke muttered.

J.T. lifted his beer in silent salute, and Jeff reached for the phone.

The telephone rang, interrupting her thoughts, and Kelly reached for it like a drowning woman grabbing at a life preserver.

"Hello?"

"Hi."

Even if she hadn't recognized his voice, the reaction of her body to that deep, rumbling sound would have told her that it was Jeff. Good heavens. He could do this to her even over the phone lines?

"Kelly," he was saying, and she drew her hormones back from the brink far enough to concentrate. "You think you could get one of your brothers to baby-sit tonight?"

"I suppose so," she said. "Why? What'd you have in mind?"

"I was thinking about taking you out on a date."

A warm flush swept over her, and her fingers curled tightly around the receiver. "A date?"

"Yeah," Jeff said, and his voice came soft and intimate in her ear. "A date."

"Uh…" she said, stalling for some unknown reason because she knew as well as he did that she would say yes. "Okay. What time?"

"I'll pick you up at seven."

"I'll be ready."

Jeff hung up the phone, then picked up his beer. Lifting it high, he waited for his friends to do likewise before saying, "Target acquired."

Nine

She should have known he'd play dirty.

Kelly steeled herself against being swayed by his tactics, but it wasn't easy to stand firm against a man like Jeff—especially when he was determined to be romantic. Especially a man you were already halfway in love with.

And he'd pulled out all the stops for their "date."

Moonlight poured down from a star-filled sky and danced across the surface of the ocean. A soft wind ruffled the sand and lifted her hair from the collar of her turquoise cowl-necked sweater. As

Jeff refilled her champagne glass, she glanced around the tiny cove and told herself he'd chosen his spot well.

This was *their* beach. The spot where he'd saved her life eighteen months ago. The place where this had all started.

In a couple of months, the beach would be crowded, even at night, with scores of teenagers. But now, this early in the season, it was deserted. The rock walls of the cove surrounded them on three sides, and high above, perched on a cliff, was a five-star restaurant. The soft strains of piano music drifted down to them and seemed to melt into the sigh of the outgoing tide.

"More champagne?" Jeff asked, ending her thoughts and bringing her back to the moment at hand.

"Sure," she said, though an inner voice was warning her to stay alert. He already had everything going for him here. The romantic setting was perfect. A tablecloth spread out on the sand, candles set in hurricane globes, their flames bobbing and shifting in the breeze, iced champagne and a caterer's tray of snacks. Moonlight glinted in his blue eyes and a shaft of pure, unadulterated lust shot through her, and Kelly knew she was in big trouble.

She had to keep her wits about her. He was using the big guns on her tonight, and if she wasn't careful, she'd find herself pillaged and captured. And right now, that didn't even sound like a bad idea.

Oh, boy.

She lifted her glass and took a sip, letting the icy bubbles slide down her throat. When she was sure her voice would work without quavering, she spoke up. "You really went to a lot of trouble tonight, Jeff."

"No trouble," he insisted, pouring himself more of the expensive wine.

She laughed and shook her head. "You set all this up, and even posted a guard on it while you came to get me." She hadn't gotten a good look at the man Jeff had waved off as they'd arrived, but he'd had the bearing of a Marine.

"That was Travis," he said, taking a drink of champagne. "Travis Hawks. He's a member of my team."

Safe territory, she thought and snatched at the subject. "Tell me about them," she said. "Your team."

He looked at her for a long minute, and Kelly knew that he knew what she was up to. But it didn't seem to matter. He shrugged and started talking. "There are three of them. Travis, Deke and J.T. We've been together for a long time. Long enough that we can each tell what the others are thinking."

"You're good friends," she said, judging more from the warmth in his tone than his words.

"The best," he agreed, giving her a soft smile. "But it's more than that. We're family."

Family. He said the single word as if it was sacred, and she knew how much that meant to him. The last time they were together, he hadn't talked much about his childhood, but he'd said enough for her to know it hadn't been an easy one. She knew he'd grown up mostly in an orphanage before being placed in a foster home when he was in his late teens. But by then, it was too late for him to forge any kind of a bond with a family situation.

He was too much his own man. Even then. Kelly had no trouble at all imagining what he'd been like at sixteeen. Tall, good-looking, with shadows in his eyes and a way of holding himself apart from everyone around him.

Which pretty much described him as he was now. Except with her. And Emily.

And the realization of that hit her hard. Family was all-important to Kelly, and she'd grown up in the loving arms of four overbearing brothers.

Though their parents were gone now, killed in a traffic accident five years ago, the five of them remained close. If family meant so much to her, what would it mean to a man who'd never really known it before?

"We've been in some hairy situations," he was saying, and Kelly forced herself to pay attention. To keep her mind from wandering down dangerous paths. "But each of us knows the others are there to watch his back."

"Tell me," she said, wanting him to keep talking, loving the sound of his voice and knowing that as long as he was talking about work, the conversation wouldn't go places she wasn't ready for. "Tell me about a typical mission."

He choked out a laugh. "There's no such thing as a *typical* mission. Every one is different." His gaze shuttered. "And I can't really talk about what I do, anyway."

"Can't or won't?" she asked.

"Both, I guess," he said, trying to be as honest as possible. "I wouldn't want to, even if I could. But most of what we do is secret. You know the old joke, 'I could tell you, but then I'd have to kill you.'"

"Charming," she said, and took another sip of wine.

"It's not an easy job," he continued, locking his gaze with hers. "But it's an important one. And I'm good at it."

"I believe you are," she murmured, watching him. Even at rest, his body was tight, as if some inner core of him were coiled, ready to spring loose into action. She had no trouble at all imagining him stealing covertly into danger and Kelly knew one thing for sure. If *she* were ever in trouble, hoping for rescue, she'd want a man like Jeff Hunter to be sent in after her.

"But I don't want to talk about the job tonight," he said. "You talk for a while."

"About what?" She didn't have anything exciting to say. No great adventures to share. She lived an ordinary life.

"About you. Emily. Your brothers."

She laughed at the tightness in his voice there at the end. "Believe it or not, they're pretty great, for brothers," she added as a caveat. "We were always a close family, but since our folks died a few years ago, we've gotten even tighter. Except for those occasions when I have to fight tooth and nail to remind them that I'm all grown up and can take care of myself."

He gave her a slow smile.

"It's nice, though," she said thoughtfully,

"having them there to count on. Our mom always told us, 'Family comes first,' and she was right. Come hell or high water, even when they irritate me beyond belief—" she paused and shook her head gently "—they're there when I need them. Just as I am for them. And that's a gift."

"Yeah," he said, his voice even tighter now. "It is."

There was something else here. Something beyond wanting to listen to her talk about her family. She just wasn't sure what exactly it was. So, trying to lighten the moment, she said, "Boy, you must be desperate for me to talk if you're even willing to talk about *them.*"

He gave her a half smile and lifted one shoulder in a quick shrug. "We didn't exactly get off to a great start, your brothers and me. But I understand where they're coming from."

"You do, huh?"

"You bet," he said, sitting up again and resting one forearm on his upraised knee. "If some clown comes dancing around Emily and leaves her alone and pregnant—" he shook his head at the thought, and the grim set of his mouth told Kelly how he'd finish that statement before he spoke and confirmed it "—I'll hunt him down like a dog."

Though a part of her warmed to hear him speak

so protectively of Emily, another part—the independent heart of her, had to say something. "Jeff, you didn't leave me alone and pregnant."

"Yeah, I did."

"Neither of us knew when you left."

"Doesn't change the facts, does it?" He tossed the last of his champagne down his throat, set the glass down and stood up. Feet braced wide apart, arms folded across his chest, he stood staring out at the black ocean, and his gaze locked on the silvery trail of moonlight that stretched out into eternity.

Kelly set her own glass down and stood up to join him. Standing directly in front of him, she placed both hands on the corded muscles of his forearms and looked up into his face. She kept staring at him until he lowered his gaze to hers.

In the glow of the moonlight, she saw the shadows in his eyes darken and gather and she wasn't sure if it was anger or pain. All she knew was that she wanted to ease those shadows back.

"You didn't know," she repeated, her voice firm.

His jaw worked and she could almost *hear* his teeth grinding. "Like I said, that doesn't change the facts, does it?"

"And I wasn't alone," she pointed out. "I

wouldn't think I'd have to remind you of that. The guys have been 'dropping by' on you all week while you've been watching Emily.''

In fact, the Rogan brothers had made a point of checking up on Jeff. Not a day went by that one of her brothers hadn't been at her house when she got home from work. And though the week had started out rough, by Friday, even Kevin had warmed up some toward Jeff.

And Kelly wasn't sure which was better—them *liking* Jeff or *not* liking him? Either way, her brothers had plenty to say to her about him.

"No, you weren't alone," he admitted, and unfolded those arms to pull her in close. "But I wasn't there. And I should have been."

Exasperation kicked in. Talk about a hard head. "Are you going to beat yourself up over this for the next twenty or thirty years?"

"What do you expect?"

"I expect you to get over it. Emily's here. My pregnancy is long done and everyone's fine."

He moved one hand to cup her cheek. "Yeah, and that's something else."

She blew out a breath, and the curls on her forehead danced. "What?"

"I missed seeing you pregnant."

Kelly laughed shortly. Frankly, she was more

than grateful that he hadn't seen her at her biggest. Call it vanity, but she knew darn well she'd been as big as a house.

"You didn't miss much," she told him. "Remember the whole 'beach ball' mental picture I drew for you a week ago?"

"Yeah," he said. "I remember. And I'm betting you looked beautiful."

She laughed harder this time and tried to take a step back. But he caught her close, wrapping his arms around her middle and holding on for all he was worth.

"Beautiful," he repeated. "You were pregnant with *my* baby. How could I think you looked anything but beautiful?"

Oh, God.

Her insides were melting.

Any minute now, she'd pool at his feet.

Jeff looked down into those fathomless green eyes and even in the dim light, he saw his future. She smiled and his heart was lighter. She scowled and every nerve in his body went on full alert.

He'd listened to her talk about her brothers, about the strength of the bond between them, and he'd hungered at the love in her voice. He'd watched her with them, with Emily, and longed to be included in the easy give and take of a family.

Even more than he had when he was a kid, standing on the outside of warmth, looking in.

Then it was just a sense of wanting to belong—
anywhere. Now he wanted to belong with Kelly. He wanted to be a part of her warm and generous heart.

This wasn't just about Emily.

He was in love. For the first and last time in his life. And he wanted it all. Desperately.

"I love you," he said, relishing the feel of the words on his tongue. He'd never said them before. Never thought to be in the position to say them. Never thought he'd *want* to say them.

But now he wanted nothing more than to say those words to her for the rest of his life.

"Jeff, don't—"

"Don't what?" he asked, still holding on to her tightly. "Don't tell you how I feel? Don't ask you to marry me?"

"This isn't about love, Jeff," she said, and bracing both hands on his chest, pushed hard in an effort to be free. But he wouldn't let her go. Couldn't let her go.

"What is it about then?"

"Emily," she said flatly. "It's about our daughter and your notions of what the honorable thing to do is."

"Maybe it started out that way," he admitted. Actually, it *had* started that way. He'd known his duty the minute he'd found out that he'd created a child. But this was so much more now.

This was everything.

"Maybe?"

"Okay, not maybe. But things are different now."

"Different how?" she demanded, and this time succeeded in pushing free of him. Her feet shifted on the sand, and she threw out her arms to catch her balance. "You don't think you have a duty to us anymore?"

"Of course I do, but that's not all of it."

She sighed and shoved her hair back from her face. "Yes, it is." Shaking her head, she smiled at him. "I don't *need* you to take care of me. I can do that myself."

"I know that," he said, and meant every word. Hell, that was one of the things he loved best about her. Her independent spirit. She was a woman who would do what had to be done and wouldn't sit around waiting for someone to come in and help. In short…she was the perfect Marine wife. "I admire that in you."

"Thanks," she said, and lifted her chin. "I had to work hard for it. I have four brothers who've spent most of my life trying to tell me what to do, how to do it and when to get it done.''

"I'm not like them.''

"You're a man, aren't you?''

"You're damn right I am,'' he countered hotly. "But I'm also a professional Marine. You think we *want* wives who can't do for themselves? A Marine needs a woman who can stand on her own two feet. Who can make decisions and pay the bills and take care of minor disasters alone.'' He drew a breath and told himself to calm down. He'd never win the day by shouting. "Hell, most of the time, Marine wives are handling cross-country or international moves all on their own. Trust me, honey. Your independence is as important to me as it is to you.''

"I doubt that,'' she snapped. "I had to fight long and hard for that independence. Now, you might mean well and all—''

"Might?''

"But,'' she went on as if he hadn't interrupted her, "I'm not going to give it up because you think you have a duty to me.''

"Duty?'' he muttered, stung. "That's what you really think? That this is about duty?'' Wouldn't you know it, he told himself, the first time he admits to loving someone, she doesn't believe him.

Somewhere, someone was getting a real laugh over this. "My 'duty' could be taken care of as easily as signing over a part of my check to you and the baby."

"I don't want your money," she said quickly.

"I *know*." He threw his hands high and let them fall back to his sides again in frustration.

"Good," she said, "I'm glad that's settled."

"Oh," Jeff told her with a shake of his head, "it's not settled." He closed the distance between them in one long step and took her upper arms in a firm yet tender grip. Pulling her close enough that she had to tip her head back to look up at him, Jeff let his gaze move over her features before saying softly, "What I feel has nothing to do with duty, Kelly."

Then he lowered his head and kissed that mouth that he still dreamed about. He tasted the woman he would never get enough of. He gave her all that he was, all that he ever would be, in a long, slow, deep kiss that seared them both with the sizzle of something rare and powerful.

At last, he broke the kiss, lifted his head and met her gaze. "So Kel, was 'duty' all you felt just now?"

Ten

Another week raced past, and Jeff was more and more aware of time slipping away from him. Two more weeks and his leave would be up. Two more weeks and he'd be off and running again.

And unless he could get this thing with Kelly straightened out before he left, he figured he'd be pretty much miserable for the next year or so. But damn if she wasn't as stubborn as she was beautiful. She wouldn't even *discuss* marriage with him. And to make matters worse, she'd decided that since she couldn't be what he wanted, that it would be better for both of them if they didn't sleep together anymore, either.

Jeff glared at himself in the mirror. "You've got a hell of a way with women," he told his reflection, and wasn't at all surprised by the scowl he saw in the glass. "Yeah," he went on, and paused to swipe his razor across his shaving-cream-covered jaw, "real impressive. Now she's not only determined to stay single, she's determined to stay celibate. Nice job."

Damn it. He'd never been so frustrated. And now he wasn't even thinking about the lack of sex. This frustration stemmed from having Kelly shut the door on the fantasies he'd been building in his mind.

All his life, Jeff had been on the outside, looking in. Until he'd found his place in the Corps, he'd thought of himself as a kid locked outside a candy store. Able to see all the goodies life had to offer—just unable to reach them. Finally, he'd given up wanting them. Given up thinking he'd find a way to have what everyone else seemed to take for granted.

Then out of the blue, he'd stumbled across it. He leaned over the sink, his fingers curling over the cold porcelain until his knuckles whitened. For all the good it had done him. Because now that he'd found it, he'd been locked outside again.

And the pain of knowing he was so close and still been found unworthy, was damn near enough to bring him to his knees. An emptiness more all-consuming than anything he'd ever known before blossomed inside him, and Jeff stared at the man in the mirror as if looking for helpful suggestions.

But nothing came. Just another wave of fatigue that crashed over him with the force of storm surf.

Man, he was so tired, his eyes felt as if they were on fire. But how could a man be expected to sleep when images of Kelly haunted him? Her face, her body, her laugh. For the past week, every time he dozed off, he'd awaken minutes later, hard and hungry and alone. Hell, he'd had more sleep during firefights.

He nicked his chin and sighed his disgust as blood welled up through the white foam. "Perfect," he muttered, and finished shaving before bothering to stop the bleeding. Of course, the shape he was in, he'd been lucky to just slice up his chin. A few more sleepless nights and he'd be too dangerous to shave himself.

The phone rang and he went to answer it, grateful to have something to take his mind off his thoughts. Slinging the towel over his shoulder, he grabbed the receiver like a man snatching at a hastily thrown lifeline.

"Hello?" he asked, hoping to hear a certain husky female voice.

"Hey, boss," Travis drawled lazily.

Jeff gripped the receiver more tightly, tamped down the rush of disappointment and sat down on the edge of the bed. Man, was his brain fried or what? Hoping for a distraction from thoughts of Kelly, then disappointed that it wasn't *her* on the phone.

"Hey, Travis. What's up?"

"Not a hell of a lot," the other man said. "Peace is boring as hell, isn't it?"

That all depended, Jeff supposed, on just how your peaceful leave was spent. If there was one thing the past two weeks *hadn't* been, it was boring. But he never had been one to share, so he simply said, "Yeah. Sure is."

"So," Travis continued in a slightly more hearty tone, "the guys wanted me to tell you that we're headed to Tijuana for the day. Thought we'd see if you wanted to ride along."

Jeff's gaze focused on the open sliding glass doors across the floor from him. Sunlight fell into the room, lying across the carpet in a rectangle of golden warmth. His brain raced as he considered his options.

Tijuana with his friends or spending a whole Saturday watching Kelly try to avoid being alone with him? Tough choice. He scrubbed one hand across his face and came away with a streak of shaving cream he'd missed. Hell, maybe the best thing for him and Kelly would be a little space.

They'd been in each other's faces for two solid weeks. And this past week especially, the tension between them had been thick enough to slice through with a bayonet.

If he went with the guys, he knew it would be easy. The bond they shared had been forged and tested in fire. They were family, and right now he needed to feel as though he belonged. Somewhere.

"Boss?" Travis prodded. "You still there?"

"Yeah," he said. "I'm here."

"Good. So what do I tell the guys? You in?"

"Sure," he said, making the decision his gut told him was the right one. "Count me in. When do we leave?"

"Deke'll be there to pick you up in a half hour."

"I'll be ready."

He hung up and stared at the phone. Now all he had to do was call Kelly and tell her he wouldn't be coming over. And hope to hell he didn't hear relief in her voice.

"So where's Recon?" Kevin asked as he took a seat on the front porch.

Kelly looked up from the flower bed she'd been attacking for the past hour and shot her brother a look. So much for peace and quiet. When Jeff had called earlier to tell her he wasn't coming over today, she'd been torn between relief and disappointment. Though she'd miss seeing him, hearing his voice, his laughter, she also needed a little time to herself to think. Which is what she'd been planning to do. Until Kevin turned up out of the blue and planted himself on the porch as if he fully expected to spend the day there.

"He went to Tijuana with his friends today."

"Good." He lifted his glass of iced tea and took a long sip.

Sitting back on her heels, Kelly tossed her hair back from her face and demanded, "What's that supposed to mean?"

"Nothing." He cradled the glass between his palms and stared off down the tree-shaded street in a not very veiled attempt to avoid meeting her gaze.

Blast it. There were just *way* too many men in

her life. Irritation swelled inside her and she took several deep breaths in an effort to calm herself.

It didn't work.

"Spit it out, Kevin," she told him flatly. "I've got weeds to kill and pansies to plant." And thoughts to think and plans to make and Jeff to miss, she added silently.

He turned his gaze back to her and stared at her for a long, thoughtful moment. "Okay, I'll say it. I'm glad he's not here. I'm tired of tripping over him every time I want to visit my niece."

Surprise rippled through her. Interesting reversal, Kelly thought. Since Emily's birth, Kevin and the triplets had been doing nothing but waiting for Jeff to show up so they could somehow force him and Kelly to get married. Now that he was here and determined to do that very thing, Kevin did an about-face?

Why was the whole world suddenly going nuts?

"All right," she said, staring at him and waiting for the other shoe to drop, "what's up with you? You're the one who was leading the 'let's marry Kelly off' parade for the last year and a half."

"The operative word in that sentence would be 'was.'"

Irritation rose up again, strong and powerful.

She looked at her older brother and blurted out, "God, Kevin, would you just say it?"

"I don't want you marrying him."

She blinked at him. Absently, she heard Emily cooing to herself and the shouts of the kids playing soccer down the street. A soft wind tugged at her curls, and she leaned forward long enough to plunge her trowel into the damp earth. Then she sat back again, dusted her palms together and faced the older brother who had sometimes been her nemesis and always been her rock.

"Why?" she asked quietly. "Why the big change of heart?"

"Simple. I changed my mind."

Kelly laughed shortly, and Kevin shot her a warning glare. "I'm sorry," she said, holding one hand up, dirty palm out. "It's just that, you changing your mind is as likely as the sun suddenly backing up and orbiting Earth in the opposite direction."

"Funny."

But true, she told herself. Kevin was the original hardhead. Maybe it came with being the oldest—but once he'd made up his mind, it was carved in stone. Until, apparently, today.

"Okay, fine," she said in a placating tone, silently reminding herself that this man had loved her all her life. She at least owed him the chance to speak his piece without interruption. "You changed your mind. Why?"

Kevin rested his forearms on his knees and looked at the lip of his glass as if it held the answers to every question ever asked. Clearly stalling, trying to get his thoughts in order, he waited what seemed forever before speaking. Finally, though, he lifted his gaze to hers. "He's Recon, Kelly. And Recon Marines are a bad bet as family men. As husbands."

Her heart ached just a little, though she couldn't have said why. She didn't want to marry Jeff anyway, right? So why should it bother her that her brother was now on *her* side of this? Was it hearing him dismiss Jeff so easily? Was it an instinctive urge to defend? The ache lingered, but she swallowed back the discomfort lodged in her throat and asked, "Why?"

"Kelly, Recon gets the dirtiest, most dangerous jobs there are."

She'd known that already. The last time Jeff was here, he'd explained to her some of his job. And the rest of her information, she'd gotten from her own research. It really was amazing what you could find on the Web these days.

She'd found enough to terrify her. Recon Ma-

rines went into hostile situations at the drop of a
hat. Alone, they slipped into trouble spots, did
whatever they'd been sent in to do, then tried to
make it out alive again.

It sounded to Kelly like a lonely job. Never being stationed in one spot. Never being able to tell
people where you were or what you were doing.
Living always on the edge, constantly checking
your back. She'd wondered all those months when
he'd been gone if Jeff had thought of her. If he'd
clung to memories to keep him company in those
dark nights when danger was too close for comfort.

A chill raced along her spine, despite the bright
warmth of the sun on her back.

"Most of the time," Kevin was saying, "they
have to leave at a moment's notice." He pointed
one finger at her. "And they can't say where
they're going."

"I know that," she said. "I'm the one who got
postcards from all over the world, remember?"
Postcards with hastily scrawled messages of hope,
longing. She'd saved every one, telling herself it
was for Emily's sake that she tucked them away.
But there was more to it than that, Kelly knew.
Even though she didn't want to admit it to anyone.
Least of all, herself.

"Postcards," he said on a snort. "That's the

kind of husband you want? Gone for months at a time? Never knowing where he is or what he's doing? Spending the rest of your life worrying?''

A flash of temper hit her hard, and she found herself defending Jeff. ''Geez, Kevin,'' she snapped. ''You act like Recon Marines are the only ones who leave families behind to do their jobs. *You* were deployed regularly until you became a drill instructor.'' She scrambled to her feet, prepared to do battle. ''And you will be again, once this rotation is over.''

''Yeah, I was,'' he agreed with a sharp, hard nod. ''And will be. But you'll always know where I am, won't you?''

''That won't stop us from worrying, though, will it?'' Hands on her hips, she leaned in toward him. Kevin set his glass aside and stood up, too.

''No, but you'll always be able to get in touch with me, won't you? You couldn't get hold of Recon when you found out about Emily.''

''If I'd been his wife, I could have,'' she countered, not even stuttering on the word *wife,* which should have surprised her. But at the moment, she was far too furious to think about it.

''Damn it, Kelly, you asked my opinion and I'm giving it to you.''

"Yes, well, now I've changed *my* mind. I don't want your opinion."

"Because you don't like it?" He leaned closer to her, reaching out one hand to grab her forearm. "Why the hell are you defending him, anyway? I thought you didn't want to marry this guy."

"I didn't—*don't*," she snapped, then shook her head and pulled away from Kevin's grasp. This was all too confusing. She didn't want to get married, but she also didn't want her brother tearing Jeff apart for doing his job. For being every bit as Marine to the bone as he himself was.

Jeff was alone. He didn't have family to pester and care. All he had was her. And Emily. A ping of something soft and sweet tinged her heart at the thought, but Kelly shook it off for now.

"I think you'd better go," she muttered thickly, trying to make sense of all the thoughts careening through her mind at breakneck speed.

"You're telling me to leave?" Kevin sounded incredulous.

"Yes," she said. "I am."

"Kelly, I'm your brother and—"

Her head whipped up, and she frosted him with a look that any of the recruits in his charge could have told him was a patented Rogan glare.

"And I'm not twelve years old."

"I didn't say you were."

"No, but you act as though you think I am. Blast it, Kevin, I can take care of my own life," she snapped. Then turning to snatch Emily up out of her walker, she plopped her daughter on one hip and gave her brother one long, last look. "Instead of being so darn conscientious about running mine, why don't you go out and find a life of your own?"

Then, leaving him staring openmouthed after her, Kelly took the porch steps quickly, went inside and closed the door on him.

When Jeff called a few hours later, Kelly's emotions were still running high. Nothing made sense anymore.

She'd never wanted a husband, but she wanted Jeff.

She wouldn't admit to loving him, but she needed him.

And the thought of his leaving again, going off into God knew what kind of danger, made her insides tremble with the force of an 8.5 earthquake.

"Kelly," he asked, his voice rumbling across the phone lines to settle in the pit of her stomach. "Are you okay?"

She shoved one hand through her hair, looked at their daughter, cheerfully mashing peas in one grubby fist, and forced a smile. "Yes, I'm fine. But I think I zoned out a minute ago. What did you ask?"

He chuckled and the sound vibrated inside her.

"I asked you to go to dinner with me. Tonight."

It had been a long day without him. She'd become accustomed to having him in her life. To seeing him every day. To hearing his voice, seeing his smile, watching him with Emily.

And all too soon, she'd be missing him again. His leave was nearly up and before she knew it, she'd be haunting the mailbox again, hoping for another card from some far-off place. Why shouldn't she spend every minute she could with him? she asked herself.

Why hold herself back from feeling his arms around her, luxuriating in his touch? Why sentence them both to loneliness before they were separated by his job?

"Hello?" he asked, prodding her gently until she realized that she'd zoned on him again.

"I'm sorry, Jeff," she said with a shake of her head. "Long day, I guess."

He picked up on that instantly. "If you're too tired, then—"

"No," she said quickly. "No, I'm fine.

And...I'd love to have dinner with you. What time?''

''Eight o'clock,'' he said, adding softly, ''wear something gorgeous.''

''Eight,'' she repeated, already mentally rummaging through her closet. ''I'll be ready.''

Eleven

The Quiet Cannon restaurant in Laguna Beach was perched high on the edge of a cliff. Its glass walls overlooked the ocean far below, and each table was turned to take advantage of the view. Soft music drifted into the restaurant from the adjoining bar, and muted conversations filled the room as waiters moved soundlessly between the diners.

"This is beautiful," Kelly said, smiling across the white-linen-covered table at him.

"No," Jeff said, his gaze traveling over her for

at least the tenth time in the past half hour. "*You're* beautiful. The restaurant's just nice."

"Thank you," she said as politely as if they'd been on a blind date and this was their first meeting. "You look very handsome in your uniform."

He winced just a bit before explaining, "It was wear the uniform or try to sneak into this place in jeans and sneakers. I didn't have any dress clothes with me."

"I'm glad," she said. "I like seeing you in your uniform. I like seeing other people's reactions when they see you."

Uniforms always did command a certain amount of attention, he acknowledged, which was why generally an off-duty Marine made it a point to wear civvies. Unless, he thought wryly, they made reservations at a swanky restaurant and *then* discovered they didn't have the right clothes.

"The people looking at us tonight aren't seeing me, baby," he said, his gaze locking with hers. "All they can see is you and they're probably wondering how a guy like me got lucky enough to be here with you."

She smiled at him and his heartbeat kicked into high gear. What he'd told her was no more than the truth. From the moment he'd picked her up at her house, he'd done little more than stare at her.

The soft, pale yellow dress she wore fit her as if it had been made for her alone. The low, scooped neck gave him a tantalizing peek at the swell of her breasts, and the short sleeves displayed her slender, tanned arms to perfection. The full skirt fell to just above her knees and swirled around her truly great legs with every step she took. She wore her curly hair pulled back from her face and swept up into a silver clip at the back of her head. A few curls escaped capture, though, and danced about her face with abandon. Candlelight glinted off her slash-of-silver earrings and twinkled off the bracelet she always wore on her left wrist.

Her green eyes practically glowed in the shimmering light, and Jeff felt as though he could sit there forever, staring into those eyes and be a happy man.

But as the waiter brought him the bill, he realized this night was almost over. And there was still so much to say.

Hell, he'd spent most of today planning what he'd tell Kelly the next time he saw her. And now that he was here, with her, all he could do was look at her like some dumbstruck schoolboy.

Disgusted with himself, he glanced at the check, dug into his pocket and pulled out a clip of cash. He counted off the appropriate number of bills, including a substantial tip, then slid out of the booth. Holding one hand out to Kelly, he helped her up, then steered her toward the front of the restaurant, one hand at the small of her back.

Pride filled him as he caught a couple of approving stares from the men they passed. Kelly was beautiful and he was happy to see that others appreciated it. But she was so much more than just a pretty face.

She had spirit and courage and pride. She had a laugh that could make a deaf man grin in response. She was tender and loving and—hell, he might as well admit it—she was *everything*.

Outside, an ocean wind immediately pushed at them, cold, insistent. Jeff took her incredibly soft white stole and draped it across her shoulders. She smiled up at him, and he was so close, so close to those lips of hers, he almost gave into the urge to kiss her.

But then the valet parking guy loped up out of the darkness and asked for their ticket.

"Not yet," Jeff said, looking from the eager boy to Kelly. He didn't want this evening to end. Not until he'd had a chance to say the things he needed to. "Come around back with me?" he asked, looking into those green eyes of hers.

"Of course," she said, and walked beside him, around the restaurant, through the shadows.

The narrow, decklike patio clung to the edge of the cliff. A few hundred feet below them, the ocean rolled toward shore. Slamming against the sand in a never-ending assault and retreat. But here, surrounded by potted flowers and the reflected glow of the candles in the restaurant behind them, they were alone, quiet.

He almost hated to shatter the spell that existed between them. But he had to say this. Had to get out all of the words that had been clawing at him all day.

"I did a lot of thinking today," he said softly, staring out at the black water.

"So did I," she answered, but didn't elaborate and he couldn't help wondering just what she'd been thinking. But then, her thoughts probably hadn't taken the direction his had.

He'd spent hours wandering around Tijuana, a tourist mecca, and hardly saw a thing. All he'd been able to think of was Kelly. And Emily. And the fact that he'd be leaving them soon. A man started looking at things—*life*—differently, when he had a child, Jeff told himself. He started to realize that he was not going to live forever. Particularly if he was in a high-risk sort of profession.

And on the heels of that thought came so many others, he wasn't at all sure he could voice them all. But maybe he wouldn't have to.

She stood so closely beside him, he felt the brush of her arm against his, and the warmth that shot through him in response shook him to his core. Her scent wafted to him on the soft sigh of wind, and Jeff inhaled it deeply, imprinting it on his soul.

Turning his head, he looked down at her and mentally captured her image forever. In the pale glow of starlight and the dance of candles scattered over the sprinkling of tables on the deserted patio, she looked like a dream. The skirt of her dress floated around her legs, and as she hugged her stole close to her upper body, she pushed the swell of her breasts higher, stealing his breath and destroying any chance at rational thought.

He looked away again, turning his gaze back to the limitless ocean.

"Kelly," he said, drawing a deep breath as if preparing for battle, "I want you to marry me."

"Jeff—"

Great job, he told himself. Bottle it up all night, then just blurt it out with no fancy words or flowery speeches. Way to go. He had to speak up again. Fast.

"Hear me out," he said, turning toward her again. "Please. Just listen for a minute."

Her gaze was suddenly shadowed, and for the life of him he couldn't figure out what she was thinking. But, since she hadn't leaped into his arms and shouted, "Oh, yes, Jeff!" he had to assume that she was still going to refuse him. With that thought in mind, he rushed through the speech he'd been practicing all day while his friends partied in Mexico.

"This isn't about us," he said, and her expression told him what she thought of that statement. "All right, not completely about us. This is about Emily, too."

"Emily?"

A twinge of something tight squeezed his heart, but Jeff ignored it and rushed on. "Damn it, Kelly, I know you don't want to be married to me," and that knowledge went down hard. Not easy on a man's pride to be turned down by the mother of his child. "But the least you can do is let me provide for my daughter."

"What are you talking about?" she asked, staring up into his face.

He grabbed her upper arms and held her firmly. God, this had all sounded so good, so easy, in his head. Why was it now, when he needed them the most, the words were nearly impossible to find? "The Corps takes care of its own, Kelly. My daughter is entitled to my benefits. To medical care. To whatever else I leave behind if something happens to me."

She blanched. He saw it despite the poor lighting, and Jeff pressed forward. "Let me do this, Kelly. Not for you. I know you can take care of yourself. But let me do what I can to help watch out for my baby."

"Oh, Jeff…"

Kelly's mind was reeling. If he hadn't had such a tight grip on her arms, she might have stumbled right over the edge of the cliff. Strange, she thought. She knew he had a dangerous job. Had been thinking of nothing else all day.

But hearing him say the words 'if something happens to me' had really hit her hard.

His features were taut. Tension rippled off of him in waves, and she knew what this was costing him. He'd put aside his pride for the sake of his child. Jeff Hunter was one of the strongest men she'd ever known. Yet he'd taken the chance of being turned down again because he was so determined to do whatever he could for Emily. Tenderness welled up inside her as she looked into those pale blue eyes of his.

"Say yes," he urged.

A part of her wanted to, and that worried her. She'd never wanted to give a man room enough to take charge of her life. She'd always prided herself on her independence. But how high a price was she willing to pay for that freedom?

Could she really say no again, knowing what it would cost him? She didn't want him leaving, going into danger, believing that he had nothing here at home waiting for him.

Kelly didn't want him to feel alone. Adrift. In the dangerous world where he lived and fought, it was important to be tethered to the *real* world. He needed to know that he mattered.

To Emily.

To her.

And he did. Whether she married him or not, Kelly knew that Jeff would always be in her heart. The magic she'd found with him a year and a half ago was not only still there, it had grown, blossomed into something so fierce, she couldn't imagine her life without it.

All day, she'd battled her feelings for him against her fear of handing her life over to yet another male. And she hadn't reached a single conclusion. Not until this moment. The moment when he'd asked her to allow him the right to provide for his child.

She couldn't deny him this. She couldn't lock him out of Emily's life.

"All right, Jeff," she said before her courage could fail, "I will marry you." She was doing this for Emily, she told herself, but even she didn't entirely believe that.

He looked so stunned, it might have been funny, but instead, it was just so blasted touching, Kelly felt a sheen of tears flood her eyes. She blinked them back, though, a moment later when he grabbed her, pulled her close and hugged her tight enough to cut off her breath.

Then he bent his head, claimed her mouth in a hard, brief kiss and when it was over, he said, "Can your brother Kieran stay with Emily tonight?"

Still dazed from his kiss, she nodded dumbly. "I think so, why?"

"Because," he said, tilting her chin up with his fingertips, "we're flying to Vegas. Tonight. Before you can change your mind on me."

"Vegas?" she repeated as he took her arm and steered her back down the path toward the parking lot.

* * *

It was all over in a matter of hours. Including plane trips and wedding service, Jeff and Kelly were back at his hotel room in Bayside before dawn.

"What are you thinking?" he asked, his voice a quiet hush in the shadow-filled room.

"Just how strange it is," Kelly mused, running her fingertips along the forearm he'd tossed across her bare middle. "A few hours ago, we were having dinner. Now we're...*married*."

He pulled her to him, rolling onto his back, trapping her there atop him, her body aligned with his. His hands moved up and down her back, over her behind and back up along her spine. The calluses on his palms sent shivers of delight across every square inch of her skin, and she had to admit that as a wedding night, this one had been legendary so far.

"No thinkin' allowed," Jeff murmured, and raised his head high enough to nibble at the base of her throat.

"Mmm..." Kelly moved into him, closing her eyes, forcing her mind to concentrate only on his touch. His kiss. He was right. No thinkin' allowed. There would be time enough later to worry if she'd done the right thing or not. For now, all that mattered was Jeff and what was left of this night.

He rolled over again, this time pinning her beneath him. Her arms came up, wrapping around his neck, holding him to her as he slid one hand up her body to cup her breast. His thumb and forefinger tweaked at her hardened nipple, sending lightning like bolts of soul-deep pleasure shooting all the way down to the soles of her feet.

Delight sizzled through her, and she wondered absently if it would always be this way between them. And then she wondered if they would have an "always." But even as that vague notion drifted through her brain, it slid out again as Jeff moved atop her, trailing his lips and teeth down her body. While his mouth tortured her, his hands skimmed her length, touching, exploring, caressing.

Every nerve ending sang. Every breath was ragged. Her mind whirled in a rush of color and sensation. She reached for him, her fingertips just skimming his shoulders as he slid lower and lower. And when he knelt between her legs and lifted her hips from the mattress, Kelly gasped and braced herself for the intimate kiss she knew was coming.

His mouth covered her and she nearly came off the bed. "Jeff," she whispered, reaching helplessly for him again.

"Enjoy, baby," he murmured, and tasted her deeply. "Just enjoy."

She did. Over and over again, his lips and

tongue swept over her most sensitive flesh and the gentle torment had her squirming in his firm grasp.

Her hands fisted in the sheets. Her hips rocked against his mouth as she fought for the release building inside her. His hands on her behind tightened as he gave her all that she could have wanted. And when the first small ripple of sensation pooled within her, Kelly dragged in one long, deep breath, squeezed her eyes shut and rode the crashing wave that followed.

But even before the last shiver had left her, Jeff was there, leaning over her, pushing himself inside her, claiming her body, branding her soul. She lifted her hips to meet his first thrust and felt whole as he entered her.

Jeff stared down into her face. "Open your eyes, Kelly," he whispered on a groan, "look at me. Look at me while I love you."

Her eyes flew open and their gazes locked, intertwined as completely as their bodies were.

"Take me, Jeff. Take all of me," she said, sliding her hands up his back, holding him to her, giving him more with her touch than anyone had ever given him before.

And as his body exploded, his last conscious thought was home. He'd finally found home.

A hideous, screeching, jangling noise broke into the silence an hour later, and still half asleep, Kelly reached blindly for the telephone. She snatched at the receiver before the blasted thing could ring again and grumbled, "'lo?"

"'Morning, ma'am, I need to speak to Gunnery Sergeant Hunter," a deep, no-nonsense voice practically ordered.

She blinked, shook her head and gave Jeff a nudge with her elbow. "Jeff," she said, pushing at him again when he barely stirred, "phone for you."

They were both practically unconscious. Flying to and from Vegas, getting married and then having a two-week honeymoon in a few hours was pretty tiring, after all.

"Yeah," he muttered, lifting his head from the pillow, but keeping his eyes tightly closed. "I'm up. I'm up."

She handed him the receiver and as he said, "Hunter here," Kelly flopped back onto her pillow.

Every muscle in her body felt like an overcooked noodle. Soft, mushy. Her brain was deliciously fogged, and if the hotel caught on fire right that minute, she'd just have to lie there and burn.

Smiling to herself at the notion, she turned her head on the pillow and noticed that even lying down, Jeff had come to attention. All vestiges of sleep were gone from his expression, and his eyes were narrowed as he listened carefully to whoever had called. A twinge of apprehension pinged inside her.

"Yes, sir," he finally said after a series of noncommittal grunts, "moving, sir."

He handed her the receiver, then rolled off the edge of the bed and jumped to his feet.

"What is it?" she asked, hanging up the phone, but keeping her gaze locked on Jeff's broad, bare back. "What's going on?"

He shot her a look over his shoulder. "Honeymoon's over, Kel," he said shortly, and stalked naked across the room toward the closet. There, he opened the door, grabbed his duffel bag and an armful of shirts off their hangers and turned back for the bed.

"You're packing?" she asked stupidly as he shoved shirts and the rest of his things into the oversize green bag.

"That was the base," he told her with a nod toward the phone. "My team's got to report in. ASAP."

"But you're on leave," she argued, sitting up and clutching the blanket to her like some sort of medieval shield.

"Leave's canceled." He walked into the big bathroom and came back out a moment later carrying a brown leather shaving kit. He zipped it closed as he walked, then tossed it into the bag.

He was actually leaving, she thought. Now. Well, she wasn't ready for this yet. "They can't do this."

Jeff actually paused in his packing, looked directly at her and gave her a quick grin. "Baby, they can do whatever they want."

"It's not fair," she said, coming up onto her knees, still clinging to that blanket with fisted hands. "You have two more weeks coming. Let them call someone else."

He laughed shortly and shook his head. "That's not how it works."

"It should be." For heaven's sake, they send him out on life-threatening missions, give him leave and then snatch it back? What was that all about? And why was she so panicked over his leaving? She'd known this was coming. Eventually. It was just that she wanted more time. More time with him.

He came around the edge of the bed, grabbed her arms and pulled her up until she was eyeball to eyeball with him. "Baby, I've got to go. That's just how it is."

"When will you be back?"

"I don't know," he said, his gaze moving over her features as if he was already committing her to memory in a silent goodbye. "But when I am, I'll get to finish this leave."

In a week? She wondered. A month? Six months? This wasn't fair and a part of her wanted to scream at the injustice of it. But her more rational side kicked in just in time.

He was a Marine. She'd known that from the beginning. And she wasn't going to send him off worrying about a brand-new wife who was clingy and weepy. Hadn't she been the one who'd been so proud of her independence? So determined to have her own life? Nodding to herself, she let go of the blanket and pressed herself to him. Wrapping her arms around his neck, she hung on tight and gave him a long, slow, deep kiss that was meant to last him as long as it had to.

And when she pulled back and looked into his eyes again, she hid the fear creeping through her body. "Go," she said softly, quietly and congratulated herself on the steadiness of her voice. "Do what you have to do, but be careful."

Pride lit his eyes, and he gave her a smile that could have blinded her. "I'll do that, baby. And then I'll be back."

Twelve

"**Mr**. Ambassador," Jeff whispered hoarsely, "keep your da—*head* down." Not a good idea to cuss at an ambassador, Jeff figured, but the man was pushing him to the limits of his patience.

It wasn't his fault he'd been captured by rebel guerrillas, but he *could* cooperate with his rescuers. Deke shot Jeff a look that said plainly he'd just as soon turn the man back over to his captors, but that wasn't going to happen.

"Sir," Travis urged in his quiet drawl, "if you'll just keep moving, we'll have you out of here in no time."

The fat, bald politician had sweat streaming down his face and a mutinous expression in his eyes. "Why isn't there a helicopter?" he demanded for the umpteenth time. "I shouldn't be expected to *walk* out of this place. I'm an ambassador!"

That did it. Jeff leaned in close to make sure the other man could see his eyes, despite the camouflage paint disguising his features. "Sir," he said, letting his voice carry every ounce of frustration he was feeling, "if you don't do what we say and get the lead out, you're going to be a *dead* ambassador."

The man sputtered angrily for a minute, then subsided. "Fine, fine. Let's just get on with it."

Just how he felt, Jeff thought and turned back to lead the way out of this pesthole. This whole mission had been a pain in the ass since moment one. Their intel had been wrong about where the captive was being held. They'd had to walk in country farther than they'd planned and now they had to fight the very man they'd been sent in to protect.

A soft snap reached him, and Jeff instantly went on full alert. Motioning to his team, he slipped off to the right, moving through the foliage with barely more than a whisper of sound. And when he came up behind the man waiting to ambush them, Jeff just as soundlessly brought the butt end of his rifle down on the man's skull.

In minutes, he was back on the trail, leading his team out of harm's way. He felt good. Sharp. Better than ever. And he knew he had Kelly to thank for it. Loving her, having a life outside the Corps had given his job more focus. Now he was more determined than ever to complete the mission safely and get home in one piece.

In finding Kelly, he'd found himself.

But a week later, he was back in Bayside, heading to Kelly's house, wondering if he was being fair to her. All through the mission, all through the escape and the trip back to safety, he'd been going over this whole situation in his mind.

Having Kelly in his life had only helped him, but what was it going to do to *her?* By marrying her, he'd sentenced her to a lifetime of worry. Was it fair to put her through countless goodbyes and long, endless nights?

No, he told himself, despite the ache that settled low in his gut. He'd waited his whole life to find the kind of love he'd dreamed of when he was a lonely kid. And now that he had found it, he couldn't claim it. For her sake. Besides, hadn't she only agreed to marry him for Emily's sake? She'd made it clear from the beginning that she hadn't wanted a husband. And he'd maneuvered her into marriage anyway. And what did that say about him?

Was he so hungry for the love that had been denied him most of his life that he was willing to put Kelly's happiness at risk? He scrubbed one hand across his face and pushed the shaft of guilt down deep inside. Selfishly, he wanted nothing more than Kelly and Emily in his life. But if he wanted the best for them—and he did, then maybe the best way to handle this was to get a divorce. Then Emily would still have his benefits, and Kelly would be free.

He frowned to himself and stopped dead on the sidewalk outside Kelly's house. Something inside him lurched at the thought of losing all he'd found in the past few weeks. But he'd never be able to live with himself if loving Kelly only brought her misery down the road.

Kelly'd spent the past week watching the news on TV and reading the newspaper far more carefully than she usually did. Not that it did her much good. It was simply amazing just how many troubled hot spots there were in the world. And Jeff could be at the heart of any one of them.

She lifted Emily off her hip and set her into the seat of her walker. The baby instantly cooed, went up onto her toes and inched herself forward.

"Look at you," Kelly said, her voice filled with pride. "Pretty soon you'll be running through the house and nothing will be safe, huh?"

Emily laughed, clearly pleased at the notion.

"I'll bet your daddy misses you," Kelly said, and took a seat in the closest chair, where she could watch her daughter while her mind raced.

The house seemed so quiet these days. Funny how she'd become accustomed to Jeff's presence so quickly. He'd become a part of their lives. A big part. And now that he was gone, she missed him more than she would have thought possible.

God, how she wished that she could talk to her mother about this—about everything that had happened recently. Though she knew darn well that her so romantic mother would tell her to grab hold of love with both hands and never let go. Pulling her knees up to her chest, Kelly sighed, wrapped her arms around her legs and tried to organize her thoughts. But it was so hard to do anything but think about Jeff and the last time she'd been with him. His last kiss. His last smile.

Her heart filled to bursting, and Kelly knew that she could no longer pretend, even to herself, that she could keep Jeff on the sidelines of her life. She'd been lost the moment she'd opened her eyes that long ago day on the beach and looked into his shadow-filled gaze. Old hurts clouded those pale blue eyes, and she knew now that she wanted nothing more than to ease back the shadows in his world. She wanted to love him and give him a home to come back to and have more children with him and enjoy all the silly, traditional things she'd laughed at when she was a "liberated" teenager.

Now, Kelly thought, she knew that if you were very lucky, you could have it all. Love deep enough to stir your soul and the independence to guide your own life.

And she was going to tell him all of this as soon as he returned. Until then, she kept busy. Running her life. Doing the things she'd always done before Jeff had crashed into her world. There were her kindergarten classes, and time with Emily and housework and gardening…any number of things to fill the daylight hours. But the nights seemed to last forever. She wondered where he was, what he was doing, if he was safe.

And she knew that that worry would be with her always. Whether she had married Jeff or not, she would have thought about him, prayed for him and worried. At least as his wife, she had a little pull with the Corps. She'd be able to find him if she had to. She'd be notified, God forbid, if anything went wrong.

Kelly jumped up from the chair as if she'd been pinched. "Nothing will go wrong," she said aloud, as if she were a child, shouting to hold off the monsters crouching in a dark room. "Jeff is good at what he does. He's careful and professional and—"

The doorbell rang, and grateful for the interruption, she walked to answer it. Pulling open the door, she stared at him blankly for a long minute before grinning and hurling herself at him. "—here. Jeff! You're back!"

His arms came around her with the strength of a vise, pinning her to him, holding her so tightly against him that she was sure in another minute or two, their bodies would just blend together. Which was all right with her.

"Hi, baby," he whispered against the curve of her neck.

His soft, warm breath sent shivers of anticipation rolling along her spine, and when he kissed her, she took his face in her hands and relished the feel of him. Warm, safe, alive.

When she came up for air, she pulled back, took his hand and drew him inside, closing the door behind him. "Why didn't you call?"

Jeff shrugged and looked at Emily, who gave him a sloppy smile that tore at his heart and weakened his knees. "It was faster to just come over."

"Well," she said, coming to his side and slipping her arm through his, "I'm all for that, then." She looked up at him, and he steeled himself to meet those green eyes that would haunt him forever. "How long do you have now that you're back?"

"I can finish out my leave. Two weeks." And after he'd said what he came to say, he didn't know if she'd be relieved or never want to see him again.

He lifted one hand and smoothed her hair back from her face. Her silver earring winked at him, and he realized how much he would miss all of the little things about her. Those earrings she was never without. The flash of her smile. The husky sexiness of her smile. The touch of her hand. The warm welcomes—like the one he'd just received. He'd never experienced that before. Never had anyone waiting for him to come back. Never really mattered to anyone before Kelly.

How he would miss belonging here. With her. With Emily.

"What's wrong?" she asked, taking an instinctive step backward. Her gaze locked on his features, he knew she was seeing the misery in his eyes. "Jeff, what is it?" She gave him a quick look, up and down, as if searching for some unnoticed injury. "Are you hurt?"

"No," he said quickly, though he was hurt far more than he would ever let her know. Walking away from her would be the hardest thing he'd ever done in his life. "I'm fine," he said. "It's just—"

"Just what?"

"I've been doing a lot of thinking this last week."

"About…?"

"You. Me. Emily."

Her expression shifted and uneasiness gleamed in her eyes. Best to just say it, he told himself. Flat out and fast.

"The thing of it is," he said, with a quick glance at his daughter, ramming her walker into the back of his knee, "I think you were right all along."

"About what?"

"About us. About how we shouldn't be married."

She blinked at him, but snapped her mouth shut when she clearly had something she wanted to say.

So Jeff kept talking, taking advantage of the silence.

"It's not fair to you," he told her, briefly bending down to turn the walker so that Emily could move around the room. "I shouldn't have dragged you into my life, Kel. I don't want you to spend the rest of your life worrying about me. I want you to be happy. Safe. So I think it'd be best if we just ended this marriage as quickly as we went into it."

A long, pain-filled silence fell over the room. Seconds ticked into minutes, and still she didn't say anything, just looked at him through green eyes stung with surprise. And just when he'd about given up hope that she was going to speak to him at all, she started in on him.

"*You* think," Kelly said, fighting past the stunned sensation clawing at her. She couldn't believe it. In all the times she'd imagined his homecoming, she hadn't pictured this little scene once. But then, who would have? Ridiculous to think that only ten minutes ago, she'd had a serious case of the warm fuzzies, planning to tell him just how much she loved him. Shaking her head, she took a step closer to him, lifted one hand and poked his chest with her index finger. "*You've* decided?"

"Yeah," he said, though his eyes looked a bit wary now, as well they should.

She shook her head on a choked laugh. "Unbelievable. This is precisely why I never wanted to get married. I didn't want some man making my decisions for me."

"This isn't like that," he tried to explain.

"That's exactly what this is," she countered, before he could even finish. "This is…amazing. Do you know, that in the last week—since they found out we got married—my brothers have actually backed off? They're not offering advice and opinions every time I turn around. *They've* finally come to the conclusion that I'm a grown-up, capable of thinking for myself. Unfortunately, it seems my *husband* hasn't gotten the word yet."

"Kelly—"

"No," she told him. "You had your say. It's my turn."

He braced himself, folding his arms across his chest and meeting her gaze squarely. "Fine. Go ahead on."

"Gee," she said, "thanks." Unable to hold still a moment longer, she started walking a slow circle around him. He followed her with his gaze, turning his head from side to side to keep up with her movements.

She wasn't sure whether to hit him or hug him. Then she took a hard look into his eyes, and the shadows haunting them tugged at her heart. He was so clearly willing to give up what they had together in order to protect her—she knew just how much he loved her. And that fact touched her so deeply, it brought a sheen of tears to her eyes. Unfortunately for him, her temper had control of the situation at the moment.

"So you think if you leave me I won't worry about you?"

"I just think—"

"*And,*" she out-talked him, "that I need protecting—I obviously am unable to care for myself."

"Now, I didn't say that exactly—" he interrupted quickly. "It's just that I know I rushed you into this and—"

"You really believe I would have *married* you if I didn't want to?" Could he actually think that she didn't love him? After all they'd shared?

He opened his mouth but she didn't let him talk.

"Oh, I told myself it was for Emily's sake," she said, warming up to her theme now, "and I let you believe that. But the simple truth is, if I didn't love you, I wouldn't have married you."

Jeff looked as though someone had hit him over the head. "You love me?"

"Yes," she snapped, then added, "but for heaven's sake don't ask me why right now."

"You love me."

He grabbed her as she walked past him again and held her still. She looked up into his eyes and saw the stunned disbelief shimmering in those pale blue depths. Was he really so surprised that someone could love him? That old pain tinged his voice, and in his eyes, she thought she caught a glimpse of the lost child still somewhere inside the strong, powerful man standing in front of her. Tenderness welled up inside her, and Kelly lifted one hand to cup his cheek. Shaking her head, she asked, "How can such a smart man be so dumb?"

He pulled her to him, holding her face between his palms. Afraid to believe, he said softly, "Baby, if we stay married—"

"If?" she questioned, wrapping her arms around his neck. She smiled at him and watched those shadows slowly fade. "Try and get away, Recon," she said. "I'll find you."

He gave her a half smile, then stared at her in all seriousness. "Being married to a Marine means moving. A lot. Different cities. Different countries."

"We'll see the world."

"I won't be able to discuss my missions with you."

"As long as you come back to me," she told him, "I won't care."

"In Recon, I'm gone a lot."

"The homecomings should be fun," she said, running her hands up and down his chest and back up to encircle his neck.

He took a breath and blew it out. "Military life can be lonely for spouses."

"I can teach anywhere. And I'm a big girl," she reminded him. "I can take care of myself."

Jeff smiled again, feeling the emptiness inside begin to lift. "I'm gettin' that."

"We're apt to fight a lot," he warned, "since I want to protect you and you want to do for yourself."

She grinned at him. "Making up is the best part of arguing."

"I can't guarantee I won't get bossy."

"And I can't guarantee I'll listen to you," she said.

Jeff's gaze shifted slightly to where his daughter was sitting in her walker, chewing on the hem of the lace curtains. "I don't know much about being a father."

Kelly followed his gaze briefly, smiled and

turned back to him. "By the third or fourth baby, you'll probably get the hang of it."

Jeff's heart ached it was so damn full, and a part of him wondered if he'd go around with this twinge of pain for the rest of his life. If so, it was a small price to pay.

"How did I get lucky enough to find you?" he whispered, his gaze moving over her features lovingly.

"That's easy, Marine," she said, going up on her toes to bring her mouth closer to his, "you saved my life one summer day. And then you made my life worth saving."

His breath caught in his chest, and a knot of emotion closed off his throat. "I've never loved anyone before in my life, Kelly. It's you. Only you. *Always* you."

"I love you, Jeff," she whispered, staring up at him, willing her to read the truth in her tear-shrouded eyes. "For now, forever."

His arms came around her then, in a viselike grip. He crushed her to him, wanting to feel all of her at once. He'd come so close to losing this. So close to never knowing what love really was. Jeff buried his face in the curve of her neck and inhaled the scent of her, making it a part of him. At last, he thought, sending a grateful prayer heavenward.

At last he'd found a place—and a heart—to belong.

"I swear, Kelly," he murmured as he lifted his head to look into her eyes, "I will love you forever. And then some."

She smiled at him through her tears and whispered, "Welcome home, Jeff," just before he kissed her.

* * * * *

Don't miss Maureen Child's next book,

LAST VIRGIN IN CALIFORNIA,

coming in October from
Silhouette Desire.

SILHOUETTE® MAKES YOU A STAR!

Feel like a star with Silhouette.

We will fly you and a guest to New York City for an exciting weekend stay at a glamorous 5-star hotel. Experience a refreshing day at one of New York's trendiest spas and have your photo taken by a professional. Plus, receive $1,000 U.S. spending money!

Flowers…long walks…dinner for two… how does Silhouette Books make romance come alive for you?

Send us a script, with 500 words or less, along with visuals (only drawings, magazine cutouts or photographs or combination thereof). Show us how Silhouette Makes Your Love Come Alive. Be creative and have fun. No purchase necessary. All entries must be clearly marked with your name, address and telephone number. All entries will become property of Silhouette and are not returnable. **Contest closes September 28, 2001.**

Please send your entry to: **Silhouette Makes You a Star!**

In U.S.A.
P.O. Box 9069
Buffalo, NY, 14269-9069

In Canada
P.O. Box 637
Fort Erie, ON, L2A 5X3

Look for contest details on the next page, by visiting www.eHarlequin.com or request a copy by sending a self-addressed envelope to the applicable address above. Contest open to Canadian and U.S. residents who are 18 or over. Void where prohibited.

Silhouette®
Where love comes alive™

Our lucky winner's photo will appear in a Silhouette ad. Join the fun!

HARLEQUIN "SILHOUETTE MAKES YOU A STAR!" CONTEST 1308
OFFICIAL RULES
NO PURCHASE NECESSARY TO ENTER

1. To enter, follow directions published in the offer to which you are responding. Contest begins June 1, 2001, and ends on September 28, 2001. Entries must be postmarked by September 28, 2001, and received by October 5, 2001. Enter by hand-printing (or typing) on an 8 ½" x 11" piece of paper your name, address (including zip code), contest number/name and attaching a script containing <u>500 words or less, along with drawings, photographs or magazine cutouts, or combinations thereof</u> (i.e., collage) <u>on no larger than 9" x 12"</u> piece of paper, describing how the <u>Silhouette books make romance come alive for you.</u> Mail via first-class mail to: Harlequin "Silhouette Makes You a Star!" Contest 1308, (in the U.S.) P.O. Box 9069, Buffalo, NY 14269-9069, (in Canada) P.O. Box 637, Fort Erie, Ontario, Canada L2A 5X3. Limit one entry per person, household or organization.

2. Contests will be judged by a panel of members of the Harlequin editorial, marketing and public relations staff. Fifty percent of criteria will be judged against script and fifty percent will be judged against drawing, photographs and/or magazine cutouts. Judging criteria will be based on the following:

   - Sincerity—25%
   - Originality and Creativity—50%
   - Emotionally Compelling—25%

   In the event of a tie, duplicate prizes will be awarded. Decisions of the judges are final.

3. All entries become the property of Torstar Corp. and may be used for future promotional purposes. Entries will not be returned. No responsibility is assumed for lost, late, illegible, incomplete, inaccurate, nondelivered or misdirected mail.

4. Contest open only to residents of the U.S. <u>(except Puerto Rico)</u> and Canada who are 18 years of age or older, and is void wherever prohibited by law; all applicable laws and regulations apply. Any litigation within the Province of Quebec respecting the conduct or organization of a publicity contest may be submitted to the Régie des alcools, des courses et des jeux for a ruling. Any litigation respecting the awarding of a prize may be submitted to the Régie des alcools, des courses et des jeux only for the purpose of helping the parties reach a settlement. Employees and immediate family members of Torstar Corp. and D. L. Blair, Inc., their affiliates, subsidiaries and all other agencies, entities and persons connected with the use, marketing or conduct of this contest are not eligible to enter. Taxes on prizes are the sole responsibility of the winner. Acceptance of any prize offered constitutes permission to use winner's name, photograph or other likeness for the purposes of advertising, trade and promotion on behalf of Torstar Corp., its affiliates and subsidiaries without further compensation to the winner, unless prohibited by law.

5. Winner will be determined no later than November 30, 2001, and will be notified by mail. Winner will be required to sign and return an Affidavit of Eligibility/Release of Liability/Publicity Release form within 15 days after winner notification. Noncompliance within that time period may result in disqualification and an alternative winner may be selected. All travelers must execute a Release of Liability prior to ticketing and must possess required travel documents (e.g., passport, photo ID) where applicable. Trip must be booked by December 31, 2001, and completed within one year of notification. No substitution of prize permitted by winner. Torstar Corp. and D. L. Blair, Inc., their parents, affiliates and subsidiaries are not responsible for errors in printing of contest, entries and/or game pieces. In the event of printing or other errors that may result in unintended prize values or duplication of prizes, all affected game pieces or entries shall be null and void. **Purchase or acceptance of a product offer does not improve your chances of winning.**

6. Prizes: (1) Grand Prize—A 2-night/3-day trip for two (2) to New York City, including round-trip coach air transportation nearest winner's home and hotel accommodations (double occupancy) at The Plaza Hotel, a glamorous afternoon makeover at <u>a trendy New York spa</u>, $1,000 in U.S. spending money and an opportunity to <u>have a professional photo taken and appear in a Silhouette advertisement</u> (approximate retail value: $7,000). (10) Ten Runner-Up Prizes of gift packages (retail value $50 ea.). Prizes consist of only those items listed as part of the prize. Limit one prize per person. Prize is valued in U.S. currency.

7. For the name of the winner (available after December 31, 2001) send a self-addressed, stamped envelope to: Harlequin "Silhouette Makes You a Star!" Contest 1197 Winners, P.O. Box 4200 Blair, NE 68009-4200 or you may access the www.eHarlequin.com Web site through February 28, 2002.

Contest sponsored by Torstar Corp., P.O Box 9042, Buffalo, NY 14269-9042.

COMING NEXT MONTH

#1381 HARD TO FORGET—Annette Broadrick
Man of the Month
Although Joe Sanchez hadn't seen Elena Moldonado in over ten years, he'd never forgotten his high school sweetheart. Now that Elena was back in town, Joe wanted her back in *his* arms. The stormy passion between them proved as wild as ever, but Joe would have to regain Elena's trust before he'd have a chance at the love of a lifetime.

#1382 A LOVING MAN—Cait London
Rose Granger didn't want to have a thing to do with worldly and sophisticated Stefan Donatien! She preferred her life just as it was, without the risk of heartbreak. Besides, what could the handsome Stefan possibly see in a simple small-town woman? But Stefan's tender seductions were irresistible, and Rose found herself wishing he would stay…forever.

#1383 HAVING HIS CHILD—Amy J. Fetzer
Wife, Inc./The Baby Bank
With no husband in sight and her biological clock ticking, Angela Justice figured the local sperm bank was the only way to make her dreams of having a baby come true. That was before Angela's best friend, Dr. Lucas Ryder, discovered her plans and decided to grant her wish—the old-fashioned way!

#1384 BABY OF FORTUNE—Shirley Rogers
Fortunes of Texas: The Lost Heirs
Upon discovering that he was an heir to the famed Fortune clan, Justin Bond resolved to give his marriage a second chance. His estranged wife, Heather, was more than willing to welcome Justin back into her life. But would Justin welcome Heather back into his heart when he learned the secret his wife had kept from him?

#1385 UNDERCOVER SULTAN—Alexandra Sellers
Sons of the Desert: The Sultans
When corporate spy Mariel de Vouvray was forced into an uneasy partnership with Sheikh Haroun al Jawadi, her powerful attraction to him didn't make things any easier! With every new adventure, Mariel fell further under the spell of her seductive sheikh, and soon she longed to make their partnership into something far more permanent.

#1386 BEAUTY IN HIS BEDROOM—Ashley Summers
Clint Whitfield came home after two years overseas and found feisty Regina Flynn living in his mansion. His first instinct was to throw the lovely strawberry blond intruder off his property—and out of his life. His second instinct was to let her stay—and to persuade the delectable Gina *into* his bedroom!

SDCNM0701